WHAT READERS ARE SAYING ABOUT THE HORSES OF HALF MOON RANCH:

"An exciting and page-turning book, perfect for horse lovers."

"A thrilling start to Horses of Half Moon Ranch. I would recommend anyone who is able to read it to do so."

"I couldn't put this book down!"

"An exciting and gripping read."

"This is the best book I have ever read. Jenny Oldfield's whole series is amazing...This story is so well described I would recommend it to all horse lovers."

"I totally love the Half Moon Ranch series by Jenny Oldfield. I've read nearly all of them and I can never put them down until I've finished them, they're so good."

"This story is one that I enjoyed. I hope that the author will continue to display such talent in writing."

"I found this book really thrilling and couldn't put it down."

"This is a good read for any horse lover. I enjoyed it a lot."

"You can fall in love with the adventurous story line, and get flown away to the Western U.S., where you will meet galloping horses under starlight. Gives the reader an interesting, always-on-the-move, adventurous, story line."

"I found this book very moving…I highly recommend [it]."

"Another great book by Jenny Oldfield."

"The best. I felt that I was there."

"Brilliant! I loved this book."

"I would recommend to any horse lover!"

The Horses of

HALF MOON RANCH

Johnny
Mohawk

The Horses of

HALF MOON RANCH

by Jenny Oldfield
Wild Horses
Rodeo Rocky
Crazy Horse
Johnny Mohawk
Midnight Lady
Third-Time Lucky

The Horses of
HALF MOON RANCH

Johnny Mohawk

Jenny Oldfield

SOURCEBOOKS
Jabberwocky
AN IMPRINT OF SOURCEBOOKS

Sourcebooks and the colophon are registered trademarks of Sourcebooks, Inc.

Published by Sourcebooks Jabberwocky, an imprint of Sourcebooks, Inc.
P.O. Box 4410, Naperville, Illinois 60567-4410
(630) 961-3900
Fax: (630) 961-2168
www.sourcebooks.com

Originally published in Great Britain in 1999 by Hodder Children's Books.

Library of Congress Cataloging-in-Publication Data

Oldfield, Jenny.
  Johnny Mohawk / Jenny Oldfield.
     p. cm. — (Horses of Half-Moon Ranch ; bk. 4)
  Summary: When a guest at the Half-Moon Ranch in Colorado becomes injured while riding a horse named Johnny Mohawk, thirteen-year-old Kirstie must prove the horse's innocence to prevent a costly lawsuit.
  [1. Horses—Fiction. 2. Ranch life—Colorado—Fiction. 3. Colorado—Fiction.]
  I. Title.
  PZ7.O4537Jo 2009
  [Fic]—dc22

                              2008039730

            Printed and bound in the United States of America.
               VP 10 9 8 7 6 5 4 3 2 1

1

"Yee-hah!" Brad Jensen galloped Silver Flash into the corral. He reined the big sorrel mare to a sliding stop, kicked his feet from the stirrups, and vaulted to the ground.

Kirstie Scott and Lisa Goodman leaned on the fence and watched the young Texan rider.

"Pretty fancy," Kirstie murmured. Brad had put the strong quarter horse through her paces on the stretch of level pasture by Five Mile Creek. He'd trotted her into the clear, shallow water, then loped her toward the ranch, raising a spray that shone like a million diamonds in the bright sunlight.

Lisa pulled down the peak of her baseball cap to shield her eyes. Brad was now hitching Silver Flash to a rail between Cadillac and Moose, his heeled boots and fringed leather chaps dripping from the charge along the river bank. "Yeah; fancy boots, fancy chaps." She was evidently trying hard not to look impressed.

"Jeez, no; I was looking at Silver Flash's footwork." Kirstie wasn't the least bit interested in the fifteen-year-old dude rider. Brad might be tall and lean, with short, fair hair and contrasting dark brown eyes, and he was a frequent visitor with his fourteen-year-old brother, Troy. But it was the horse who stole her attention. "For a big mare with a long stride, she sure can turn and stop on a silver dollar!"

"...As Hadley would say." Lisa grinned and jerked her head toward the old wrangler who was the chief help at Half Moon Ranch. Today was Sunday, the start of a week's vacation for a bunch of twenty or so paying guests. It was time for Hadley Crane's introductory talk.

"Now, y'all need to respect your horse," Hadley was

telling the group. "Don't go kicking him too hard or dragging at his mouth to get your own way." He stood by the door of the tack room beside a board with a list of horses' names chalked on it. After the talk, he would allocate a horse to each guest by asking a few brief questions and choosing a mount to suit the rider.

The nervous first-time visitors bunched together at the gate to the corral. They had flown in from cities in the East. Most worked in offices, schools, and hospitals and had never seen the snow on the peaks of the Rockies or the sparkling, blue-green mountain lakes except in holiday brochures and on TV. Many had never been on a horse.

Hadley's gaze flicked coolly from one to the next. "Click, don't kick," he told them in a low, slow drawl. "When you want your horse to walk, click your tongue at him. When you want him to trot, click again."

"Hey, Kirstie. Hey, Lisa!" Brad Jensen ignored the talk and came to lean on the fence next to the girls.

"Hey," they murmured back without looking at him.

"What's the instruction when you want the horse to canter?" a man at the back of the group asked Hadley. The speaker was short, middle-aged, and slightly built, dressed in jeans and a white polo shirt. His voice didn't sound American.

"You English?" Hadley asked.

"Irish," came the reply.

A boy of about Brad's age stood next to the man, looking as if he wished he was somewhere else.

"What d'you reckon—father and son?" Lisa whispered. The man and boy looked alike, with the same wavy dark hair and light gray eyes.

"Yep." Kirstie had already glanced at the list of guests. "Paddy and Stevie Kane from Macgillycuddy Reeks, County Kerry."

"*Macgill-y*...what?" Brad twisted his tongue around the strange name.

"Hey," Kirstie warned, "I want to listen to Hadley!" She didn't, but she wanted Brad to shut up.

"Well, now, here in America, we don't canter; we lope," the ranch hand drawled. "And when we ask our horse to lope, we give him a kissing sound."

"*Kiss, kiss!*" Brad's brother, Troy, came up from behind, lunged at Lisa, then swung his

4

leg over the top rail. He straddled the fence and jammed his white Stetson down over his forehead, ready to laugh and joke his way through Hadley's talk.

"Yuck, Troy!" Lisa complained. She pretended to wipe her freckled cheek.

"'*Yuck, Troy!*'" he echoed.

Brad grinned. "Kiss the horse, baby brother, not the girl!"

"Not this girl, leastways!" Tossing her auburn curls, Lisa made a show of walking off through the gate into the corral.

Kirstie followed. "Pity the poor horse," she muttered. Troy and Brad were OK as far as horsemanship skills went, but as people, they got on her nerves.

"Troy's on Yukon for the week, right?" Lisa stopped beside the pretty brown and white appaloosa mare tethered along the row from Silver Flash and gave her a sympathetic pat.

"Right." Kirstie tuned in again to Hadley's talk. She noticed that the Kane father had chosen to stand to one side since his question about loping. He'd folded his arms and taken on a superior frown, as if he'd heard it all before. The son, however, had stayed with the group.

"When you're out on the trail, we want you to take care of yourselves," Hadley went on, stepping down from the boardwalk outside the tack room and into the middle of the bunch. "We ride in a line...that's single file to you folks from Ireland...and we don't pass the horse in front, 'cause that's gonna upset that other horse a little bit."

The group parted to let the wrangler through. He paused beside a couple of teenage girls who were staying with their parents at Brown Bear Cabin on the road out toward Hummingbird Rock.

"So, how long have you folks been riding?" Hadley asked them.

The girls, Carole and Linda Holgate, let the wrangler know that this was their first time at a dude ranch. Scanning the list of names, he chose two quiet, steady quarter horses who'd been in the remuda at Half Moon Ranch since Sandy Scott had set up the business five years earlier. Then he moved on briskly to Stevie Kane.

"Howdy, Stevie." Hadley went through the routine,

one eye on the names on the board. "You ridden Western before?"

"You bet your life he ain't!" Brad Jensen's loud remark was followed by a hoarse laugh.

Kirstie saw Paddy Kane bristle and step up beside his son.

"No, sir!" Troy crowed. "He learned to ride English back home, you bet!"

"So?" Lisa turned on the Jensen boys. "Riding English is harder than riding Western, if you wanna know!"

Troy rode the six-foot-high fence as if he was on a small, high-stirruped English saddle. "Oh, yeah; *cant-ah, cant-ah!*"

Ignoring them all, Kirstie turned to look at Charlie Miller, Hadley's young assistant, who was leading a dainty black horse into the corral, ready to be tacked up for the first trail ride of the week. Johnny Mohawk, the five-year-old stallion, was acting up as he came through the gate, pulling at his lead rope and tossing his long, dark mane.

Kirstie smiled to herself. Trust the half-Arab to make a grand entrance, as usual. She studied the high-stepping walk, the slim legs; the arched neck, flaring nostrils, and large, dark eyes of the lively horse. Johnny was beautiful from the tips of his ears down every inch of his muscular, shining body to the tips of his polished hooves. And didn't he just know it!

Charlie gave him a second to calm down, then steered him clear of the other horses, leading him to a post by the barn door. He tied him securely and strode across the corral, past the bunch of visitors, into the tack room for Johnny's bridle and saddle.

"Hey!" Brad stopped fooling to take a good look at the new arrival. He came up close to Kirstie to quiz her. "Where did he come from?"

"What do you mean?" Walking across the corral toward Johnny, hoping to leave Brad behind, she muttered a moody question in answer to his pushy demand.

"This black horse; he wasn't here last year." Brad circled Johnny Mohawk, taking in the horse's aristocratic good looks. "Jeez, he's a nice-looking brute. Where'd you get him?"

"From a film unit that was working out here last fall." Proud of Johnny, she found herself explaining to Brad, reaching out to stroke the horse's soft cheek and velvety muzzle. "He was a stunt horse in a movie, along with a dozen or so others. The horse trainer sold five of them after they finished shooting. Mom saw him in the San Luis sale barn, fell in love with him, and brought him back here."

Johnny Mohawk tossed his head and stamped his foot, as if he knew they were discussing him.

"Yeah, we know you're a beautiful boy!" With a grin, Kirstie took a bit and bridle from Charlie and began to fit the tack. "The problem is, *you* know it, too!"

"...How about the black Arab?" a harsh voice cut in, and a figure strode across the corral.

Stooping to peer under Johnny's neck, Kirstie spotted trouble ahead in the shape of Paddy Kane.

The Irishman had spotted Johnny Mohawk and wanted him for his son. "This is a good mount for Stevie," he insisted. "A horse with a bit of spirit is what he wants, not some plodding old time-server."

"I'd say Crazy Horse was the right horse," Hadley was insisting without seeming to contradict too strongly. "Crazy Horse is smart, and he knows the trails."

"It's OK, Dad, I don't mind." Lingering behind the two men, Stevie offered a way out. "The chestnut looks fine to me."

"But this black one has a definite touch of class." Paddy Kane walked around Johnny Mohawk as Charlie finished saddling him. "You don't want an ugly ride like the chestnut. You want something that looks right!"

Kirstie frowned and turned her back to buckle Johnny's cheek strap. Plodding? Ugly? The mouthy little guy knew nothing! Out of the corner of her eye, she saw her mom come across the yard and stand quietly by the fence.

"Well, now, are you sure your boy could handle Johnny?" A hint of scorn had edged into Hadley's voice.

"My boy can handle any horse you've got on this ranch!" The boast drew attention from all corners of the corral, while Stevie himself dropped his head in embarrassment. "Didn't you know? We run our own trekking center back in Kerry, so the boy was practically born in the saddle. He was riding by the age of eighteen months, following in my footsteps, hacking out in the Macgillycuddy

Mountains, helping me break in new horses. You're not telling me that this black horse is too much of a handful for the likes of us!"

Hadley listened, then sniffed. "You folks have Arab horses in Kerry?"

"Connemaras, cobs, hunters, Arabs; any type of horse you care to name!"

"Dad, it's OK!" Stevie tried again to break the deadlock between the two men. He seemed to hate having the eyes of the whole corral on him and his big-headed father.

"Shut up, son. I want this week in the Rockies to be a challenge for you. I'm paying a lot of money for it, and I insist on the very best horse they've got!"

"How about letting Stevie give Johnny Mohawk a try, Hadley?" Sandy Scott had climbed the fence and dropped into the corral. The breeze caught her fair hair and rippled through her bright, blue and white checked shirt. Her tanned face and gray eyes gave no sign of irritation. "He can ride Johnny out along Five Mile Creek this morning. I'll be leading that ride, so I can keep an eye on him."

"Sure." Although visibly angry, Hadley still did as his boss told him. Turning and striding back across the corral, he made sure that Carole and Linda Holgate were happy with their mounts.

"Hmm." Paddy Kane grunted and nodded without a word of thanks.

Sandy nodded kindly at the red-faced Stevie. "You need to know that Johnny Mohawk is a little different from the rest of the quarter horses here," she explained. "It's partly his pedigree and partly his recent history. If I tell you that Johnny's been in the movies, that should help you understand!"

"Wow, a movie star!" Now that the argument between the two stubborn men was settled to Paddy Kane's satisfaction, Brad Jensen began to joke and fool around once more. He jumped up onto Silver Flash and wheeled her close to where Stevie Kane stood. "Johnny Mohawk belongs to the Hollywood brat pack!"

"I know who's the real brat around here!" Lisa sidled up to Kirstie and watched the other guests mount their horses.

Sandy took the time to hold the black horse still while Stevie swung into the saddle. "He likes to be looked at and admired, that's all," she told him.

"You'll see his head go up when he joins the others and he begins to show off a little."

Sitting deep in the big Western saddle and gathering the reins in his left hand, Stevie nodded. "I can handle him. Don't worry."

No sooner had he said that than Johnny Mohawk seemed to set out to prove him wrong. The gleaming black horse felt the boy's weight in the saddle and must have picked up the fact that this was the first time that Stevie Kane had ridden Western style. Sitting back on his haunches before the rider's feet were in the stirrups, he launched himself across the corral in a quick, edgy trot. Stevie jerked backward and grabbed the saddle horn. He hung on to it with his right hand as he hooked his feet through the stirrup irons, then reined Johnny back. After three or four steps, he was upright and in control, laying the reins to the left to avoid Carole Holgate and her sister, using his legs to steer the horse neatly toward the gate.

Kirstie had stepped back to stand beside Lisa and watch horse and rider go. She saw Johnny Mohawk arch his neck and carry his tail high, saying *Look at me!* as he trotted across the corral.

"The kid's good!" Lisa sounded surprised. Stevie and Johnny came to a neat halt at the head of the line waiting for Sandy Scott to take them off along the creek trail. "Like, he's new to Western, but he sure knows how to bring Johnny into line!"

Once at the gate which faced the track along the green valley between the steep mountains of the Meltwater Range, the stallion tossed his head and skittered sideways, keeping his rider on his mettle. When the Jensen brothers came up on Silver Flash and Yukon, loudly jostling for position, he ducked his head and kicked back hard. Once more, Stevie Kane had to make a grab for the saddle horn and hang on.

"But not *that* good!" Kirstie said quietly.

Kirstie and Lisa saw Sandy ride to the front on Jitterbug. Quickly, they ran for Lucky and Crazy Horse so they could to join the end of the line behind Paddy Kane on big, creamy white Cadillac.

Ahead lay the blue and gold of larkspur and dandelion meadows and the rainbow spray of white water rapids cutting through granite. There would be beaver dams and elk coming down to drink—and, if they were lucky, the scamper of striped chipmunks along felled pine-tree trunks.

"Yee-hah!" Brad gave his cowboy yell as they all set out eagerly on Five Mile Creek Trail.

2

Kirstie sat easy in her saddle. Ahead of her, the line of horses and riders was soon strung out along the riverbank, shaded from the hot sun by stands of aspen trees. Their delicate, silver-green leaves shimmered in the breeze.

"Easy, Lucky!" Holding back her palomino horse, she smiled wryly as she saw Crazy Horse take it into his head to settle Lisa in behind Paddy Kane and Cadillac. The two horses went everywhere together, which was bad luck for her friend.

"At my riding school in Kerry, we have a horse-walking machine to provide the animals with exercise," the talkative Irishman was telling Lisa proudly. "And we have an indoor arena with an all-weather surface."

"Gee."

"Of course, we insist on helmets for all our riders."

"Yeah?"

"The law demands it in Ireland. And all my staff have advanced first-aid diplomas, though we naturally put safety first, so their expertise is rarely put to the test."

"Sure." Lisa sighed and glanced back at Kirstie with a look that said, *Boy, is this guy boring!*

Kirstie grinned at the narrow escape for her and Lucky. Instead of listening to Paddy Kane, she could do what she loved best when she was out on the trail, which was to drift off into a world of her own. First she let her gaze rest on distant Eagle's Peak, snow-capped even in midsummer. Then, closer to the track, she caught sight of small herds of mule deer amongst the ponderosa pines. If she stayed well back, there would be no talking, no having to be nice to guests; that was her mom's department.

Up ahead, she noticed Sandy Scott slowing down to show the riders the safest place to take their horses across the fast-flowing creek.

Skunk cabbage growing in the boggy ground at the water's edge, delicate calypso orchids in the shade of the aspens, marsh marigolds, crimson paintbrushes, wild roses, and carpets of blue columbine, the Colorado state flower: Kirstie was busy making a mental list of all the flowers she'd seen on the trail so far.

"Yee-hah!" Brad and Troy broke into her thoughts by charging into the water together.

Yukon and Silver Flash plunged shoulder deep into the cold current, churning up spray as they went.

"Hey!" Linda Holgate protested at the sudden soaking.

Troy stood in his saddle, took off his Stetson, and whooped and yelled some more. Yukon braved the swirling water and plunged on ahead of Silver Flash. The plucky appaloosa climbed the far bank with water streaming from her brown and white flanks.

"Easy does it!" Sandy coaxed on the two worried Holgate girls, watching their cautious progress and waiting for the other guests to follow. "C'mon, Stevie, you gotta let Johnny Mohawk know who's boss here!" she called to the Irish boy who was still hovering on the bank. "He's a horse who doesn't like to get wet!"

"Aww, it spoils his movie-star image!" Troy Jensen jeered. "Where's his stuntman? It ain't written nowhere in this horse's contract to swim a river; no, sir!"

Ignoring the raucous yells, Stevie clicked and urged Johnny forward. The black horse drew back his head and shuffled sideways, sending loose stones sliding down the bank. Stevie clicked again and gave a smart kick with his heels. This time, Johnny Mohawk did respond. He deigned to put one hoof in the water, then lifted it and backed off.

"Go on, make him do it!" Paddy Kane broke from position beside Lisa, his face set in a bad-tempered frown. Ignoring Sandy Scott's protest, he took Cadillac down the bank and leaned sideways to grab Johnny's rein, ready to haul him forward. But the black horse resisted harder than ever. He pulled away, lost his footing on the rocks, and began to slide.

"Whoa, easy!" Stevie flung out his free arm in the

struggle to keep his balance. He went with the skid, trusting Johnny to find his feet and leaning well back in the saddle. The horse hit the water, steadied himself, and plunged on. The rapid current buffeted him, swirling and foaming at shoulder height as Stevie gave him a loose rein and let him make his own way across.

"Nice riding!" Sandy turned her back on the boy's father and encouraged horse and rider up the far bank. Then, in another show of displeasure, she rode ahead of Paddy Kane and into the river with Jitterbug. "Kirstie, watch out for Mr. Kane!" she yelled over her shoulder as she trotted to the head of the line once more.

Kirstie knew there would be no problem about Cadillac crossing the creek, and sure enough, the strong white horse had soon made it to the opposite bank. Being the last rider to cross, along with Lisa, Kirstie raised her eyebrows.

"Huh!" Lisa shook her head and gave a shudder. "Fathers!"

Kirstie laughed. "C'mon, you can't say that about all of them!"

"I can about mine!" Lisa rode on out of the river.

Her dad had left her and her mom, Bonnie, when Lisa was eight years old.

This time there was no smile on Kirstie's wide mouth but a guarded look in her gray eyes. She and Lisa had a lot in common; her father had split up the family, too, which was the reason her mom had shut up the Denver home and brought her and her brother, Matt, out to Half Moon Ranch in the first place. But she wasn't ready to brand all fathers as no-good bullies and bores.

Only Paddy Kane.

"...Of course, Stevie is used to Connemara ponies and Thoroughbreds," he was telling Lisa as the trek continued toward the shore of Deer Lake. "It's the big racehorses he prefers to ride these days, but Connemaras are great little jumpers. I'm training young Stevie to be a steeplechaser over the hurdles. He should be ready to begin racing in a couple of seasons. He already has cups and ribbons from local competitions for young lads, you know..."

"Hum...yeah...yeah?" Lisa punctuated the drone of the man's voice, while at the head of the line, Sandy gave permission for Troy and Brad to leave the trail and lope up through the pine trees.

21

"Y'all see that pink rock up the hill?" Sandy pointed to a granite boulder jutting out on the horizon half a mile away. "That's Whiskey Rock. We can bushwhack away from the creek and meet up there in ten minutes, OK?"

"Great!" Lisa jumped at the chance to split off from Paddy Kane. She reined Crazy Horse up the slope and set him off from a walk straight into a lope, ducking low branches and weaving her way up the hill.

"...Stevie's riding ability has always been way ahead of other kids of his age." Mr. Kane didn't seem to mind that no one was listening. He went on and on as Kirstie and Lucky trotted past. "A great rider, and he's going to make a big success of his career as a jockey, just as he promised his mother he would..."

With a slight squeeze of her legs, Kirstie urged Lucky into a lope. The palomino's hooves thundered over the soft bed of pine needles; saddle leather and stirrups creaked, the wind caught her fair hair and told her she was free. Free to ride like the wind, *with* the wind, *on* the wind. Lucky's feet pounded, Kirstie ducked and swayed as branches loomed ahead. As they raced past Carole Holgate and made ground fast on Stevie Kane and Johnny Mohawk, the last thing Mr. Kane had said sank in: "Stevie's way ahead... great rider... a big success... promised his mother..."

Lucky came up alongside Johnny Mohawk, matching him stride for stride. Kirstie saw Stevie Kane's face grow tense as Johnny decided to take on the palomino in a race to Whiskey Rock. The half-Arab didn't like to be beaten, so he lengthened his stride to a full gallop, tearing up the soft ground, weaving recklessly between trees.

"Go on, Stevie!" his father called from the trail below. "You can do it!"

"Ride him, Kirstie!" Troy and Brad chorused. "Yee-hah!"

As the two horses raced neck and neck for the horizon, those words from Mr. Kane stuck with her. What had happened to Stevie's mother? Why had the boy sworn to succeed as a jockey when, as far as Kirstie could make out, he was only an average horseman?

Lucky surged forward and overtook Johnny Mohawk in the final strides of the race. Kirstie reined him back as his hooves hit solid granite and wheeled him around to face the horse and rider who had come second.

The kid had given everything; she could see it in the set of his jaw, the concentration in his brown eyes. He'd tried his best and lost. Stevie Kane; good, but not that good. A great rider? Never!

Maybe it was to cover up his defeat in the race that, for the rest of the morning's ride, Stevie Kane seemed to turn into a younger version of his dad.

"Riding English gives you much better control of your horse!" he told Linda Holgate, showing her how to post a trot. He rose in and out of the saddle, his back straight, his legs flexing to the rhythm of Johnny Mohawk's springy step.

"How come you don't stay put in the saddle?" the small, pretty, round-faced girl wanted to know. She was having enough difficulty with the Western style sitting-trot as it was, bouncing up and down and from side to side as she tried to keep up.

"Posting a trot makes it easier on the horse," Stevie explained. "Of course, you need better balance to begin with."

"Oh, sure!" Brad Jensen rode by, feet out of the stirrups.

"Yeah!" Troy followed, dropping Yukon's reins, folding his arms, and letting the mare choose her own route down from Whiskey Rock.

"Ignore them!" Lisa advised, deciding to try Stevie's upright style of trot. She soon picked up the rhythm and began to rise and fall in the saddle. "Hey, how am I doing?"

"Don't come up so high," Stevie told her. "Think of pushing forward with your hips each time."

"*Ooo-ooh!*" Brad and Troy exaggerated the movement, then almost fell out of their saddles with laughter.

Coloring deep red, Stevie urged Johnny Mohawk ahead to demonstrate. He executed a perfect posting trot along the flat stretch of meadow that led to Half Moon Ranch.

"Watch out for elk!" Brad yelled.

"And moose!" Troy echoed. "Moose are real mean!"

Stevie went ahead; up-down, up-down: the model English-style trot.

"Or bear!" Brad warned with a hooting laugh.

"Bear?" Linda gasped. She looked in alarm to the left and right.

"Sure. There are black bears in the Meltwater Range. Didn't you know?" Troy enjoyed the reaction. He swung one leg over the saddle and sat back to front, arms folded, studying Linda's face. "Fifteen at the last count; one female and two cubs over on Eagle's Peak, if you want to know."

Brad let Silver Flash head butt Yukon out of the way and came up alongside the scared girl. "Hey, no problem. Black bears are at least 95 percent vegetarian! They won't eat you—not unless you're crazy enough to get between them and their cubs. And then you're history!"

"And then you're *breakfast!*" Troy insisted, coming from behind to sandwich Linda tight between him and his brother.

Her eyes wide, breath coming short, Linda nodded. "Thanks. I'll try to remember that!"

"Troy Jensen, hand on your heart, have you ever seen a bear on Half Moon territory?" Lisa challenged. She'd given up the attempt to follow Stevie Kane's fancy trot and rejoined the main group. Meanwhile, the Irish boy and Johnny Mohawk continued to show off as they reached the bridge that led to the ranch.

"So?" Troy swung around to face the right way. He bounced in the saddle in an overdone imitation of Stevie; up-down, up-down, shoulders back, nose in the air.

"So take no notice," Kirstie advised Linda. She backed up Lisa's advice, feeling cranky and out of sorts.

True, they'd got through the morning ride without a crisis, yet she felt it hadn't gone well. The group hadn't got along, and Stevie Kane was still putting Johnny Mohawk through his fancy paces, getting him to sidestep and prance, sending a *Look at me!* message loud and clear to the beginners in the party.

Naturally, Johnny didn't need any encouragement to enjoy being the star of the show. His head was high, his neck arched; he was telling them all how beautiful he was with his dished profile and deep, dark eyes.

"...Kirstie?" Lisa broke into her disgruntled daze. "I said, can I please call my mom when we get back to the ranch and ask if I can stay over tonight?"

"Sure." She and Lucky had picked up speed to get to the corral and help Charlie and Hadley to unsaddle the horses. "Any particular reason?"

"Loretta and Wayne Stewart are coming out from San Luis," Lisa reminded her. "It's Sunday, remember? Square-dance night!"

"Red rock!" Wayne Stewart cried.

The music stopped on the prearranged cue, and everyone on the dance floor grabbed the nearest person to inflict a hug. Lisa grabbed Stevie Kane and flung both arms around him.

"That's the *real* reason you wanted to stay over!" Kirstie hissed as the music started up again, Stevie moved on to a new partner, and the girls met in the middle of the square.

"So?" Lisa didn't try to deny it. She did a neat do-si-do without letting the Irish boy out of her sight. "I'll take Stevie, thanks, and leave Troy Jensen all for little you!"

Kirstie let her mouth fall open as Charlie took her by the waist and swung her around. "Yeah, thanks!"

"What? Troy's a hunk!" Forming an arch with Matt Scott, Lisa let Kirstie and Charlie sidestep underneath. The banjo players tapped their pointed, cowboy-booted toes and quickened the tempo.

"Right!" Kirstie let go of Charlie's hand. The girls moved on to the next set. Soon, they would have to meet up with the Jensen boys.

"Anyway, Stevie Kane's cool," Lisa insisted; four steps to the right, four to the left, do-si-do and spin on the spot.

"You think so?" Kirstie couldn't see it herself. As far as she was concerned, there was something—she didn't know what—not quite right about the Kane father and son.

"He's got nice blue eyes."

"Gray!" Kirstie corrected.

Lisa dodged past Troy Jensen's set, one eye on the musicians, trying to time things just right. "Gray, blue; whatever. Anyway, he's got fabulous long lashes!"

"Lashes?" Kirstie had lost her position, floundered, and come face to face with the awful Troy. She had to admit that she'd never noticed the length of a boy's eyelashes in her entire life.

"Red rock!" Wayne cried as the music suddenly stopped.

An eager Lisa lunged at Stevie before Carole Holgate could grab him, while, to Kirstie's horror, the worst thing came to pass: she found herself lost in the tentacle grasp of Troy Jensen's dread embrace.

3

Monday morning meant serious riding. Guests were split up into beginner, intermediate, and advanced riders, then taken off by the wranglers on trails to suit their abilities.

"Make sure you're with the advanced group, Stevie!" Paddy Kane was striding around the corral giving orders. "Watch out, girlie!" he called to Carole Holgate as Charlie untied Johnny Mohawk and handed him over to the Irish boy. "Check that girth strap, someone. It looks loose to me!"

"Cinch," Kirstie said quietly, looking down from the saddle. Didn't this man ever mind his own business? "Over here in America, we call the girth strap the cinch."

Mr. Kane took no notice. He watched Charlie check the strap and say that it was OK. Then Stevie mounted and rode Johnny to the gate.

"You're not riding this morning?" Sandy Scott asked. She was gathering her intermediate group, ready to set off for Hummingbird Rock.

Paddy Kane shook his head. "I have phone calls to make, work to do," he said in his self-important way.

"Jeez, that's a real shame!" Lisa muttered out of the corner of her mouth.

"Shh!" Kirstie hid a smile by guiding Lucky around the edge of the corral, taking care to steer well clear of a grinning Troy Jensen. She could still hear Kane droning on as she and Lisa reached the gate.

"...This isn't a holiday for me. I'm here to develop my international business interests."

"Hey, Stevie!" As a bright and breezy Lisa edged Crazy Horse close to her favorite dude, Kirstie deliberately dropped back.

"Hi." He ducked his head and pretended to adjust the cinch buckle, evidently glad when Charlie rode by to head the small group of experienced riders out through Red Fox Meadow and up the forested slopes of Eagle's Peak.

"You folks ready for a tough ride?" the young wrangler asked, glancing around at Troy and Brad, Lisa, Kirstie, and Stevie Kane. "We climb up into the snow. You all got gloves and thick jackets? The wind's pretty cold at ten thousand feet."

"Yeah, yeah." The Jensens were eager to leave.

"This is an all-day ride. You need to pace it nice and slow. Don't tire your horses, and don't try any fancy bushwhacking shortcuts off the main trail." Not to be hurried, Charlie steered his horse Rodeo Rocky out onto the trail, pulled the brim of his white Stetson well down to shade his eyes, and gave the order to begin.

They were off, through the meadow, up into the shade of the aspens and pines. Today, seeing that Lisa was busy with Stevie, Kirstie chose to keep Lucky up at the front of the line, tucked in behind Charlie. She breathed in the sharp sap of the ponderosa pines, where animal claws had scratched at the bark, kept a lookout for beaver dams across the cascading mountain streams, and drifted off into her silent world.

"Lisa found a new friend?" Charlie broke in once or twice as they climbed higher and he glanced over his shoulder to see the red-haired girl deep in conversation with the Irish visitor.

"Hmm." Kirstie resisted the urge to turn and look.

"Hey, how about you and Troy at the square dance last night?" The wrangler gave a grin and a knowing look.

"*Puh-lease!*" Kirstie sighed and clicked Lucky on up a rocky stretch of trail, glad of the distraction when they crossed a track and saw the forest ranger's pickup truck parked close by.

"Hey, Smilie!" Charlie greeted the ranger from Red Eagle Lodge. Smilie Gilpin was a stocky man in his forties with thinning, fair hair and the look of a permanent outdoors life in his weather-beaten, ruddy complexion. "What's new?"

"Not a lot." The ranger walked along the track, nodding to each of the riders, ready to exchange news. "I got a couple of recreational vehicles parked up at the lodge. Nice people; a family from New England, and one from Washington. They had a scare last night, though."

"What kind of scare?" Kirstie asked.

"A bear scare!" Smilie made light of the incident. At the same time, it was obvious he wanted to pass on a warning. "You hear about the black bear and her two cubs? Well, they took a liking to the contents of the trash cans outside the RVs."

"They raided the garbage?" Kirstie's eyes widened. It was the first time for ages that she'd heard of bears bothering visitors.

"You can't blame them. Untidy trash is a treat for a hungry bear; apple cores, leftover chicken, you name it."

"What happened?" Charlie wanted the details.

"It was the middle of the night. One of the kids wakes up, looks out of the window, and comes face to face with Mama Bear! Kid starts to yell, Mama Bear opens her mouth and shows her teeth, gives a couple of snorts."

"Wow!" Brad Jensen pictured the scene.

"What then?" Troy, too, had enjoyed the description.

"Big mistake!" Smilie explained. "Instead of letting

the bears finish their supper, brave dad inside the RV decides to go out and scare them off. The next thing he knows, Mama's on her hind legs, swatting the air with her giant claws, making sure he keeps away from her cubs. I hear the guy yelling and shouting, rush out of my cabin just in time to see him step right back inside and slam the door in her face."

"So no one got hurt?" Charlie heard Smilie out, then asked his advice. "You reckon it's safe to carry on up to Eagle's Peak today?"

The guard nodded. "Sure. Bears mostly sleep during the day. And they're not aggressive, provided you don't interrupt their feeding."

"Maybe that's a point your man from the RV should have known." The wrangler gave a wry grin. "You hear that, everyone? Bears are in the neighborhood. Keep a lookout, and make plenty of noise as we go so we don't surprise them."

"No problem!" Brad turned Silver Flash back onto the trail. He gave a couple of "yee-hahs" and pushed on up the mountain, quickly followed by Troy.

Thanking Smilie, Charlie regrouped.

The ranger nodded toward the Jensen boys. "You got your hands full."

"No problem!" With a smile and a wink, the wrangler echoed Brad. "It don't matter if they ride ahead; they're advanced riders, so they know what they're doing. They just like to fool around."

Soon, Charlie, Kirstie, Lisa, and Stevie hit Eagle's Peak Trail again, climbing steadily but failing to make any impression on the lead that Troy and Brad had on them. They felt the stiff breeze gather force, seeing the tall, thick ponderosa pines thin out into twisted, gnarled krummholz, which grew in weird goblin shapes seemingly out of bare rock. Just ahead lay the snow line at eleven thousand feet.

Kirstie zipped her fleece jacket around her chin, spotting the two wayward riders bushwhacking through the trees. "The Jensens are way out of line now," she muttered to Charlie. "They're too far away for us to call them back."

"Yep." He didn't say much as he decided to take the rest of the group after them. "We'll pick up the trail again after we catch up with the boys."

"Maybe we shouldn't leave the trail in the first place." Stevie Kane looked uneasy at the idea. "If

Brad and Troy are stupid enough to get themselves lost, so what?"

"So, if we lose them up here, they're in serious trouble," Charlie explained. "Rule number one: don't let the group split up!"

"And if we follow them and we all get lost, what then?" Stevie watched the two Texan boys ride along a ridge on the near horizon. Beyond them, the triangular shape of Eagle's Peak loomed sheer and sparkling white.

"We trust our horses to get us unlost," Charlie said sharply, making up his mind and setting Rocky off across country. If he didn't act now, the Jensens would be well out of sight.

So, despite Stevie's doubts, the group took a zig-zagging path through boulders and battered spruce trees, gaining a little on Brad and Troy, then losing them behind a shadowy stretch of sheer granite. The wind grew bitterly cold, blasting down from the snowy peak in the distance, whirling occasional gusts of light snowflakes into their faces.

"This is mad!" Stevie hadn't stopped complaining in ten whole minutes. Now he left Lisa and trotted alongside Charlie, gesturing back the way they'd come. "You realize what's happening here? Those two up ahead are in danger of getting us seriously lost ten thousand feet up a mountain!"

The wrangler nodded, then grimaced. "You got a better idea?"

"There are bears around!"

"Sure. Like I said, we got a problem." Determined to keep going, Charlie pushed on.

"If it snows any harder, we'll lose the trail and never get back on!"

"I know it."

"And you still think we should follow them?" Stevie sounded incredulous. With a panicky look up ahead, he reined Johnny Mohawk to a standstill.

"Yep. I reckon Brad and Troy will be up past that stretch of rock, waiting for us."

"Yeah, really?" Stevie refused to move. He held Johnny on a tight rein. "I don't think so. And to be honest, I don't care!"

"C'mon, Stevie!" Lisa urged. "Charlie's right. You know Brad and Troy; they're most probably playing a practical joke."

"Not funny!" He was having trouble controlling his horse as Johnny strained at the bit to follow the wrangler. Hooves were beginning to slip and slide as tempers frayed.

Kirstie shook her head and turned away. The slope was too steep, the weather too bad to stop and have arguments. "He's scared to go on," she muttered to Charlie. "I reckon you gotta let him go back down."

"I'll go with him!" Lisa volunteered to help with a way out of the difficult problem. "I don't care about the rest of the ride onto Eagle's Peak, honest!"

I bet you don't! Kirstie felt a stab of jealousy. Since when did Lisa give up one of her favorite all-day rides so easily?

"I'm not moving!" Stevie continued to threaten, helping Charlie make up his mind in the process. "I'm not risking my neck for those two idiots. In fact, I'm turning right back and heading for home!"

Charlie frowned and bit his lip.

"I'll go!" Lisa insisted, taking Crazy Horse a few unsteady steps back down the rocky slope. It was against the horse's instinct to split away from the main bunch.

"OK." The wrangler gave in. "You take him onto

the trail and let your horses find their way down, you hear?"

Lisa nodded. "No problem!"

"You tell them back at the ranch that we're carrying on with the ride!"

"We'll tell them you let two crazy fools get us seriously lost in a blizzard!" Stevie retorted.

Charlie watched carefully as Crazy Horse and Johnny Mohawk turned on the narrow trail. Soon, the two breakaway riders were on their way. Though advanced, the group had broken the first rule of trail riding, and he'd failed to prevent it.

"I'll make sure my dad hears about this!" Stevie called.

Slumping slightly in the saddle, Charlie pushed Rocky on up the mountain, with Kirstie and Lucky close behind. "...Whatever!" he sighed.

By early afternoon, the snow had eased, and the sky turned deep blue in every direction. Kirstie and Charlie had long since caught up with Brad and Troy, and, after an ear-bashing from Charlie, the four of them had enjoyed the thrill of riding above the snow line along the frozen shore of Eden Lake.

"Hey!" Brad whooped and cried as Silver Flash plunged knee-deep into a snow drift. The sorrel horse floundered and struggled out again, snow caked to her sides.

"Use the trail!" Charlie reminded him. "Some of those drifts go down more than twenty feet!"

"It's hard work for the horses." Kirstie felt Lucky's flanks heave in and out as he drew breath in the thin air. Ploughing through snow made the going slow and difficult.

Whizz! A snowball from Troy grazed her cheek. *Thud!* A second landed square on her shoulder.

Kirstie scraped the icy snow from her sleeve. "OK, Troy, you asked for it!" Leaning sideways, she swept snow from a nearby branch and shaped it in the palm of her hand. Within seconds, she had returned fire. The snowball flew straight and true, catching the brim of the boy's hat and tipping it sideways.

"Good shot! Me and Kirstie against you and Charlie!" Brad yelled at his kid brother.

For a few minutes, the four of them charged along the shore, dodging enemy missiles and stopping behind trees to scrape up fresh snow and stock up their own snowballs.

"Ouch!" Kirstie cried as Troy got his revenge. Chunks of snow slid beneath the collar of her fleece and melted down her back.

"Gotcha!" Brad surprised his brother from behind.

Through it all, the horses loped gamely, churning up snow beneath their feet.

But in the end they were exhausted. Their legs slowed, their sides heaved, and they breathed clouds of steam into the crystal-clear air.

"OK, enough! Ten hits each!" Charlie declared a draw and decided that they should call it a day. He told them that he wanted to cut short the ride, head for home, and make sure that Stevie and Lisa had made it back to the ranch as planned.

"Aww!" Troy curled his lip.

"That ain't right!" Brad protested. "You said this was an all-day!"

"And it would have been if you two hadn't messed things up," Kirstie reminded them. She too felt an edge of worry about the two riders. "Next time, we stick together, OK?"

Grumbling about "the British kid" ("Irish," Kirstie reminded them), the group backtracked down

Eagle's Peak Trail, coming down below the snow line and into the dense forest where Smilie Gilpin had his ranger's lodge.

"Seen any more bears lately?" Troy called cheerily to a family sitting on camp chairs outside their gleaming silver RV.

"Not funny, Troy!" Kirstie picked up the pace. Being attacked by a black bear was no joke.

The family couldn't have heard, because they nodded and smiled and waved as the four horses rode by.

"Hey, what happened to the sun?" Putting on a show for the bemused campers, Brad did the trick of swinging around in the saddle to face Silver Flash's tail. He pulled his Stetson over his eyes and rested his legs along the horse's rump. Good as gold, Silver Flash trotted steadily on.

"Crazy!" Kirstie murmured. But she smiled to herself. The Jensen kids were over-the-top but good fun in small doses.

"Bears! Make a run for it!" Troy yelled from behind. He overtook Kirstie and Charlie at a gallop, crouched over the saddle, holding the reins high, and urging Yukon on as if lives depended on it.

"You look like the guy carrying the mailbag in an old cowboy movie!" Kirstie yelled. She let Lucky take up the challenge of a final race into the valley and along the side of Five Mile Creek. The two horses arrived in the yard together.

"Dead heat!" Troy proclaimed. He slid from the saddle with a broad grin.

Kirstie nodded back. She decided to walk Lucky around the yard a couple of times to cool him down, heading first toward Sandy Scott, who had just come out of the house to greet them.

"You're back early," Sandy said, looking up at Kirstie with one hand shielding her eyes from the afternoon sun.

"Yeah. Charlie wanted to check up on Stevie and Lisa." She glanced into the corral, looking to see if Crazy Horse and Johnny Mohawk were tethered there.

"*What about* Stevie and Lisa?" Sandy was careful to keep her voice down as they spotted Paddy Kane coming out of his cabin and making his way down the hill.

"They already got back, didn't they?" Kirstie frowned at the empty corral.

"What do you mean, they got back?" Alarm crept into Sandy's voice.

"...They didn't?" Gradually, the truth dawned. Mr. Kane drew near. He was heading for Charlie, demanding to know what had happened to his son. "They split up from us!" Kirstie whispered. "They should've been here hours ago!"

"Split up!" Paddy Kane exploded as, across the yard, Charlie explained. "You let them go off alone, without a guide?"

Sandy Scott closed her eyes and took a deep breath. "Oh, Charlie!"

"I don't believe I'm hearing this!" Mr. Kane gave an exasperated bellow and looked around furiously for the ranch boss. "You get that? He expected them to find the trail in the snow, then make their own way home!" Wagging his finger, he strode across to where Sandy stood. "I warn you, if anything's happened to Stevie out there on the mountain, I'll sue you and your precious ranch for every last penny you've got!"

4

"It wasn't Charlie's fault. It was my idea, and anyway, Stevie refused to go any farther!" Kirstie tried to get the message through to Paddy Kane.

"Yeah!" Troy Jensen did his best to back her up, while Brad took charge of Yukon and Silver Flash.

"I don't care whose idea it was. The wrangler has the final word. It's his job to keep the whole group safe; a fact which Charlie-boy here seems to have overlooked!"

"I'm sorry, sir. I was relying on the horses to find the trail and come right on home." Charlie spoke in a low, quiet voice, glancing guiltily at Hadley, who had come out of the tack room to hear the bad news.

"It seems to me you were between a rock and a hard place," the head wrangler acknowledged. He turned to appeal to Sandy Scott on Charlie's behalf. "You remember I didn't reckon Johnny Mohawk was the right horse for the kid from the start."

"Now don't you go blaming my boy for this!" Paddy Kane turned on Hadley. "We're talking negligence on the part of an inexperienced wrangler, and what do you do? You try to shift the blame elsewhere!"

"Let's cool it, shall we?" Sandy stepped in between the two older men. "Look at the facts. What we know is that for some unknown reason, Stevie and Lisa have been held up. It could be they're lost, plain and simple, or—"

"Or there's been an accident!" Paddy Kane refused to let her finish. "If my boy's hurt, I'm calling my solicitor in Killarney and getting him to draw up a case for negligence!"

Kirstie stared openmouthed at the irate father. *Forget the ambulance and the hospital*, she thought with a cold shiver. *Call the attorney!*

"There was that loose girth strap for a start!" Striding across the corral and out onto the start of Eagle's Peak Trail, Mr. Kane looked across the meadow and recalled his earlier criticism of Charlie. "If I hadn't spotted it, this wrangler would have let Stevie set off without even checking it!"

"Charlie did check it. It wasn't loose," Kirstie muttered to her mom. "And anyhow, I saw Stevie fiddling with the buckle after we left."

Sandy Scott nodded. "We're jumping ahead too fast," she insisted. "What if there's been an accident, but it's not Stevie, it's Lisa who's been hurt?"

Kirstie felt a shock run through her body at the new idea. It was true; it could be her friend who was in trouble, after all.

But then Hadley cut in. "Listen!" he warned. "There's a horse heading this way!"

They strained to hear the hoofbeats, standing at the fence around Red Fox Meadow, scanning the hillside. Kirstie saw moving shadows everywhere —under the aspen trees, beneath rocks—but no horse, until suddenly, Johnny Mohawk appeared out of nowhere. His silky black mane and tail flew in the wind, his head was high, his eyes stared as he pounded toward them.

"Stop him!" Paddy Kane yelled, standing in the horse's path and waving his arms.

Johnny's reins hung loose, he trailed a lead rope along the ground, and his heavy stirrups beat against his sides as he galloped. When he saw the figure, arms raised, shouting angrily, he whirled and reared up, hooves flailing.

"Something bad got into him!" Charlie gasped, his face pale with worry. He moved to catch hold of Johnny's reins, but the rearing horse pawed the air, making the wrangler duck to avoid the heavy blows.

"He's exhausted!" Kirstie saw the patches of sweat on Johnny's shoulders and flanks, the foaming corners of his mouth. How far had he galloped before he reached home? Where was his rider? What had happened to Lisa? Still nothing made sense.

But the first task was to catch the runaway horse. Hadley moved in quietly, past Paddy Kane and Charlie, waiting for Johnny to finish rearing, speaking in a low voice, then herding him toward the corral where he knew he would be able to corner him.

Johnny's ears flicked toward the calm wrangler, listening to him, gradually quietening, slowing to a trot inside the corral, then to a walk, and finally coming to a standstill. His eyes were on Hadley. He was lowering his head, breathing hard, still agitated but not backing away as the old ranch hand eased closer.

"Whoa, boy, nice and easy!" Slowly, Hadley raised his hand. He took hold of the trailing lead rope and moved in smoothly. Then he stroked and spoke into the ear of the quivering stallion.

"Get a rug from the barn," Sandy told Charlie as Hadley worked quickly to unfasten the cinch and take off the saddle. "Kirstie, once Johnny's untacked, walk him around the corral, give him a chance to unwind."

Following orders while her mom dealt with Mr. Kane's fresh barrage of questions, Kirstie took the lead rope and led Johnny at a steady, calm walk. He was hot and edgy, flicking his ears this way and that, rolling his eyes at every new sound. When Charlie came with the rug and flung it over his back, he flinched and pulled away as if an enemy had jumped him.

Yet, in spite of his agitation, Johnny was the one who now warned them that Lisa and Crazy Horse were on their way.

He and Kirstie had reached the far edge of the corral overlooking the creek when he dug in his heels and refused to go on. He raised his head and stared out with a fixed gaze. *Listen!* he said. *Here comes the answer to all your angry man's questions!*

"Crazy Horse!" Kirstie tethered Johnny to the fence, climbed it, and ran out into the meadow. She'd never been so relieved to see the pale tan horse's ungainly gait. He thundered across the grass, short legs pounding, heavy head hanging, carrying Lisa to safety.

"Gosh, Kirstie!" Lisa reined Crazy Horse to a sliding stop. Then she tumbled out of the saddle. "You might look as if you're glad to see me!"

Kirstie helped her to stand upright, then took Crazy Horse's reins. "Believe me, I am! Are you OK? What happened? Where's Stevie?"

"You want the bad news or the good news?" Lisa took in the group of anxious faces gathered by the corral fence. She saw Johnny Mohawk pulling at his tether, trying to rear and break free.

"The good!" Kirstie could hardly wait for her to spill it out. "C'mon, Lisa!"

"Stevie's hurt, but he's gonna be OK!"

"Hurt? How bad?"

"I think he broke his arm. And he cut his head, but don't worry, he's conscious." Lisa had obviously rehearsed her message on the ride home.

"Oh, Mr. Kane's gonna love this!" Kirstie groaned.

"He's gonna love that his son broke his arm?" Lisa frowned.

"Yeah; don't expect him to care about Stevie!" She grabbed her friend's arm and stopped short of the corral, where Johnny Mohawk still kicked up a fuss at their approach. "Come on, Lisa, spit it out. If this is the good news, what's the bad?"

Lisa drew a deep breath and stared at Kirstie with troubled eyes. "The bad news is that the horse bucked and threw Stevie off," she told her. "This whole thing is because of Johnny Mohawk; it's 100 percent his fault!"

"OK, tell me again!" Kirstie needed a clear picture of what had happened. She was out on the trail with Lisa, leading her mom and Mr. Kane, who crawled behind them in the pickup truck. They were working against the clock, letting Crazy Horse find the spot where Stevie had had his accident before daylight faded and dusk closed in.

Wearily, Lisa shook her head. "Kirstie, I already went through this a hundred times!"

"But I want to hear it without Mr. Kane jumping in and blaming everybody." She spoke low and urgently. "Take it from where you two split off. You say you got more and more lost on the mountain?"

"Yeah. I was OK on Crazy Horse here; no problem. Sure, I was cold, but I did what we always do…"

"You cowboyed-up!" Kirstie gave Lisa a sympathetic smile. Cowboying-up was the phrase they used when things on the trail got tough. There was no point moaning and crying; you just had to get on with what had to be done.

"Yeah!" Lisa grinned back. As she reached a landmark tree casting its long, deep shadow across the track, she reined Crazy Horse to the right and set off cross country. The four-wheel-drive truck bumped and rattled over the rough ground. "OK, we were lost and cold. Stevie and I—well, I guess we had a difference of opinion."

"You had a fight?"

"Not exactly. He wanted to go one way along a ridge. I reckoned we should head down to a stream."

"How did you know? I thought you were both lost."

"We were. I just felt Crazy Horse knew what he was doing, and Crazy Horse was the one who wanted to cross the stream."

"What about Johnny Mohawk?" Kirstie wanted to know.

"He wanted to come with Crazy Horse and me. But Stevie was stubborn. He held Johnny back and made him head for the ridge. I watched them until they were out of sight, not knowing if I should follow. Stevie was pushing Johnny hard, and by this time, the horse was tired. I reckoned he would have a problem if they just kept going around in circles. In the end, even though Crazy Horse didn't like it, I went after them."

"But before you could catch up with them, Stevie had his accident?" Kirstie wanted to fix the order of events in her mind. Looking around and spotting a rocky ridge ahead, she reckoned that they'd almost reached the place where Stevie Kane had fallen.

Lisa nodded. "I was riding around the pointed rock up there, taking it easy because the track gets kinda steep and scary. I heard Johnny acting up, like he was refusing to move, and Stevie was saying, 'Go ahead, go on, git!'"

"Did he kick him? Did he use the rope?"

Lisa sighed. "You asked me that before. How do I know? I couldn't see them because of the rock. But I heard Johnny snort and stamp. He sent little rocks sliding and rolling down the hill toward Crazy Horse and me. He began to whinny and squeal. He must have been bucking like crazy, because there was this avalanche of stones, and Stevie was yelling louder and louder, then Crazy Horse and me came around the corner just in time to see him flying backward out of the saddle. He hit the ground hard, Kirstie. I heard his head smack against a rock!"

"Lucky he didn't knock himself out." She glanced around to point her mom and Mr. Kane in the direction they should go next. "Almost there!" she promised.

"He could've killed himself. Anyway, he fell with his arm twisted under him. I got to him quick as I could. I raced Crazy Horse along the ridge. There was blood all down Stevie's face, but he was trying to sit up, so I knew he wasn't too bad."

"What about Johnny? What did he do?"

"He didn't hang around. Once he'd bucked Stevie off, I didn't see him because of the dust. Leastways, I was too busy trying to help Stevie to care about the horse."

"This bucking," Kirstie said, realizing that Johnny Mohawk had done the sensible thing and headed straight for home. She was still eager for precise details. "Did you actually *see* Johnny Mohawk buck Stevie off? Or did you just see Stevie fall?"

"I told you; I heard it but I didn't see it." Lisa hesitated at the tall finger of rock she'd described to Kirstie. Around this corner, they would find the injured boy. She drew a deep breath to prepare herself. "What are you saying?"

"Nothing." Kirstie clamped her mouth shut and leaned forward to pat Lucky. "Go ahead. I'll follow."

"No, wait. Are you saying that Johnny Mohawk didn't buck Stevie off after all?" Lisa hissed.

Behind them, Paddy Kane slammed the truck door and came running.

"No... I don't know!"

"You are! You're saying that Stevie's lying!" Lisa's voice rose.

"Stand clear and let me through!" Paddy Kane demanded, pushing Kirstie and Lucky dangerously close to the edge of the ridge. "Let me see my son!"

Kirstie allowed him to barge by, then leaned forward in the saddle to bring Lucky away from the steep drop.

"I'm not saying he's definitely lying!" she whispered back to Lisa, as, one after the other, she, Lisa, and finally her mom rounded the corner.

They saw Stevie Kane sitting against a rock, his right arm tied in a makeshift sling, his face white in the shadows and streaked with blood. He'd heard their voices, the truck's engine, and the sound of hooves approaching; he knew help was on its way. Kirstie would have expected him to be relieved, to have struggled to his feet to show them not to worry, that he was OK. Instead he sat quite still, staring up at his father's face.

"If you're not saying Stevie's telling a lie about Johnny, what *are* you saying?" Lisa muttered as she and Kirstie dismounted on a ledge of rock and waited for Paddy Kane to speak to his son.

Kirstie's frown deepened. What was that look in the kid's gray eyes? Was it fear of being lost and injured, of lying there helpless while coyotes, bobcats, and even bears prowled nearby? Or was it fear of his father? "I'm saying something weird is going on here," she told Lisa. "Something real weird that none of us understands!"

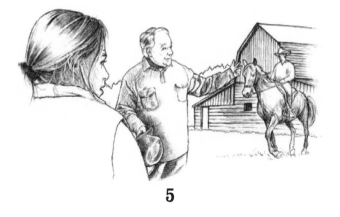

5

"Johnny just went crazy!" Stevie Kane repeated the phrase over and over as Sandy gave him first aid.

The sun had sunk behind the mountain, leaving them to rescue the boy in the cold, creeping half-light. It made Stevie's face extra pale; the blood trickling from the cut on his head seemed almost black as Kirstie's mom took pads of cotton wool from her first-aid kit. He winced as the cold disinfectant on the pad touched the wound.

"He went crazy for no reason; just reared up and dipped back down. He bucked me right off!"

"Easy, son!" Paddy Kane glanced down at the steep slope that fell away from the ridge where the accident had happened. He pointed to the churned-up ground. "A couple more steps to the right, and they'd have gone over the edge," he muttered.

"It wasn't my fault!" Stevie managed to grit his teeth and not cry out as Sandy worked on the cut. He cradled his hurt right arm, wincing with pain as he tried to shift his position. "The whole thing came out of nowhere. The horse has a mean streak, that's all!"

"Sure, Son." The father walked down the track a little way and back again, as if looking for pieces of evidence that he could store in his memory and relate to his lawyers. He stooped to pick up the riding crop that Stevie had carried, then poked at the nearby bushes with the toe of his boot.

Standing to one side with Lisa, Kirstie shook her head. It could be the pain that made Stevie sound so scared, but that still didn't mean he had to go overboard in blaming Johnny Mohawk. She thought he was protesting too much, trying to convince himself, as well as his dad. "Are you sure there was nothing on the track that spooked Johnny?" she asked quietly as Sandy finished covering the now-clean cut with gauze and tape, and then snapped shut the lid of her first-aid box. She offered Stevie a hand to stand up.

"No way!" He shot back the answer, then groaned at the pain in his arm. "That horse isn't normal. There was no reason for what he did!"

Paddy Kane stepped forward to help his son to his feet. "Don't worry, we know this wasn't your fault."

Do we? Kirstie thought. She wanted to stop this whole thing, like you could pause a video, run it back, and replay it from the beginning. And she wanted a clear camera angle; something other than Stevie's word for it.

"Have you got ahold of him?" Sandy asked Mr. Kane, checking that Stevie was steady enough to keep his balance. She waited for Kane to get in position and offer support, then headed down the track toward the pickup. "I've got a two-way radio in the car. I'll call the ranch and get Matt to call the emergency room at San Luis Hospital so they know we're on our way. We'll drive straight down there with Stevie while the girls ride back home!"

"You hear that, Stevie?" With one arm around his son's waist, the man took the boy slowly down the track. "We'll get this arm X-rayed and fixed as soon as we can. No more riding for you this holiday!"

Stevie glanced at Lisa as he limped by. Kirstie noticed that look in his eye again: a pleading, secretive, unspoken message that didn't fit the situation. "Thanks for fetching help," he muttered.

"That's OK," Lisa breathed. "Sorry it took so long. It must have felt like forever!"

Stevie took a deep breath and attempted a feeble joke. "Only when the sun went down and the coyotes started howling!"

"Coyotes?" Paddy Kane picked him up sharply, ready to list this among the other traumas his son had suffered.

"Joke, Dad!" Stevie sighed and got ready to limp down to the truck where Sandy Scott was waiting. "See you later," he told Lisa.

Together, Stevie and Paddy Kane made their way past the pointed finger of rock, disappearing in its shadow, then emerging onto the level ground where the truck was parked.

Lisa watched them climb in and slam the doors. The pickup truck eased onto the trail, its red taillights winking. Then it drove off steadily. "What's gonna happen now?" she said quietly as she and Kirstie went to fetch Lucky and Crazy Horse.

Taking a last look around at the tall pines silhouetted pitch-black against the inky sky, hearing the wind gust down the rocky slopes, Kirstie sighed. "You want the bad news, the really bad news, or the really, really bad news?"

Lisa's grin held none of its usual sparkle. "The bad news."

"OK." Kirstie mounted Lucky and turned him down the empty track. "What's gonna happen is: Stevie's out of it for the rest of this week, so Paddy Kane will ask for his money back for the whole vacation."

Up on Crazy Horse's back, Lisa clicked the willing horse into action. "And the really bad news...?"

"...Is that no way will Mr. Kane be happy with just a refund. He'll be looking for money to pay the hospital bills, more money to compensate for Stevie's injury, mega-money to show the whole world it's our fault!" And it would be thousands of dollars—the kind of sum her mom didn't have. Plodding down the track in the dim light, Lucky skittered sideways as a ground squirrel scuttled out of a bush. "But I guess maybe Matt and Mom have fixed it so we're insured for that kind of thing. So the really, really bad news is what bothers me most."

Lisa held Crazy Horse back until Lucky had righted himself and continued on his way. "Which is...?"

"...Which is what's gonna happen to Johnny Mohawk after this."

"Because Stevie's blaming him?"

"Yeah; because he's calling him crazy and mean, which I know he's not!" Kirstie's voice rose. "Because Stevie and his dad claim he's a great rider, which we know he's not!" She glanced over her shoulder at Lisa, waiting for a response. But none came. "And because at the end of all this, they're gonna say Johnny's no good for a dude ranch. They're gonna want to get rid of him!"

That Monday evening, Lisa stayed over at Half Moon Ranch. She rolled out a mattress in the corner of Kirstie's room and crept into a sleeping bag while Kirstie lay in bed looking out of the window at the dusting of silver stars in a clear night sky.

Together, the girls waited for the phone to ring.

"That was Mom from the hospital!" Matt shouted up the stairs. "She says they X-rayed Stevie Kane's arm, found a clean break of the ulna, put it into a plaster cast up to the elbow, no problem!"

Lisa scrambled out of her sleeping bag onto the landing. "What about the cut on his head?"

"Three stitches," Matt reported. "They're gonna keep him in overnight to check for concussion. Mom and Mr. Kane are on their way back right now."

"He's gonna be OK?" Lisa wanted to know.

"Fine. No need to get uptight. Try and get some sleep." Matt told her it was late.

"How late?" Kirstie mumbled as she heard Lisa crawl back into her bag.

"Half past midnight." After a long pause, as they lay with eyes wide open staring out of the window, Lisa whispered Kirstie's name, then, "Hey, I know you're thinking about Johnny Mohawk..."

The black Arab: the graceful snaking of his neck as he turned his inquisitive head, the fineness of his long, silky mane, the brightness of those intelligent, dark eyes... "Yes," Kirstie sighed.

"And you're not thinking about Stevie…" Lisa went on.

True; Kirstie had closed her mind to the slight, dark-haired, troubled kid. She didn't care about his injuries, could only hear his voice criticizing the horse, shifting the blame…"No," she confessed quietly.

"Kirstie, I'm gonna tell you something to do with Stevie that he talked to me about earlier."

Kirstie turned in bed and stared across the dark room at Lisa. "Would he want me to know?"

"Maybe not," Lisa admitted. "I got the feeling I was the first person he'd talked to since it happened. But it does make a difference."

"In how I see him?" Kirstie still wasn't sure she wanted to know. Right now, it was plain and simple. In the contest for sympathy between Stevie Kane and Johnny Mohawk, the beautiful horse came out the clear winner.

"Yeah. It's about his mom," Lisa pressed on. "She died."

Kirstie sat up and drew her knees toward her chest. "When?"

"Spring this year. She'd been sick for a long time.

Stevie says he can hardly remember a time when she wasn't sick."

"He promised her he would be a great jockey, a steeplechaser!" Kirstie said quickly, as Paddy Kane's early remark came slamming back to the front of her head. She hugged her knees and rocked forward.

"Kind of. How did you know that?" Lisa was surprised.

"His dad told me."

"Well, the way Stevie tells it, Mr. Kane was the one who gave the promise. It was one of the last things he told Stevie's mom before she died, because he knew how much Stevie's riding meant to her. That was what she'd always wanted him to do, and I guess he thought it would make her happy."

"Was Stevie there when his dad gave the promise?" Kirstie's feelings swung this way and that. How crazy for a father to do that if it wasn't what the son wanted. Yet who knew what anyone would do in that situation? You'd probably say anything, do anything for the dying person. Yes, she could understand why Paddy Kane had done it.

"Yeah. He told me his mom kinda turned to him and smiled. Stevie didn't see her again after that."

"Is riding horses really what he wants to do with the rest of his life?" If Kirstie asked *herself* the big question, the answer would be a giant yes. Horses, horses, horses! But she realized she was lucky. Hardly anyone she knew was this sure.

"I guess. I didn't ask." The darkness and the stars made Lisa's voice sound echoey and distant. "But Stevie did tell me that his dad fell apart when his mom died. He didn't care about anything, he let his business go all to pieces, hardly left his room for weeks and weeks. He only came here to Half Moon Ranch because it was a vacation that Stevie's mom had planned last Christmas when she still thought she could get better."

Kirstie sighed. "That's so sad." And yet... she still couldn't forgive the Kanes over Johnny Mohawk. And she marveled that the quiet, almost secretive Stevie Kane had opened up to tell Lisa all this.

"Before...well, before, you know...Stevie says his dad used to be a nice guy. He didn't get angry all the time, he didn't put any pressure on him the way he does now."

"Yeah, I get the picture." Another sigh escaped as

Kirstie recognized that she had to feel sorry for both the Kanes. Why was life always so complicated?

"...I thought you should know." Lisa wound down, let the pauses lengthen. "So you can understand why Stevie has to prove he's good when he's up in the saddle...Better than good, because of the promise..."

"Yeah," Kirstie interrupted. "Johnny Mohawk has gotta be wrong. Stevie's gotta be right. Because Stevie's got to be better than good. Stevie's got to be a great, great rider!"

No one had told Troy Jensen that there was a problem with riding Johnny Mohawk. The hotheaded Texan kid had gone straight out to the remuda early next morning, when the dew was still heavy on the grass in Red Fox Meadow. He'd brought Johnny into the corral and saddled him, and now Kirstie came out of the ranch house to find him practicing tricks in the neighboring round pen before Charlie or Hadley noticed what he was doing.

Troy knew how to make Johnny turn on the spot. He could circle him to the right and to the left, get him to pivot on front legs and back. Feeling the expert command of bit and heels, the Arab willingly picked up his elegant feet and did dainty pirouettes.

"Turn him, cowboy!" Troy's big brother, Brad, called from the gate, unaware of Charlie running across the yard. "Hey, look at Johnny Mohawk spin!"

The worried young wrangler pushed Brad to one side and ran into the round pen. "Take Johnny back to the meadow before the boss comes back and sees you!" he called.

Troy reined the black horse to a standstill, letting the dust settle around them. "How come?"

"Sorry, Troy. Sandy gave orders not to saddle him up today." Holding Johnny's head, Charlie waited for the kid to dismount.

"No, it's OK, I can ride him back," Troy muttered. He'd been enjoying himself in the pen, aware of the Holgate girls looking on from the corral.

"Just watch him," Charlie warned, reluctant to let go of the rein.

"It's OK, he ain't no trouble."

No, but here comes trouble! Kirstie said to herself as she saw her mom drive her car through the ranch gates. She knew Sandy had driven Paddy Kane into San Luis at dawn to collect Stevie from the hospital. This must be all three coming home now. The car swooped down the drive and pulled up in the yard.

Troy Jensen rode Johnny out of the high-fenced pen just as Paddy Kane stepped out. The boy was still showing off to Carole and Linda Holgate, proving his point to Charlie that the horse would do exactly as he was told. He rode him from a walk to a trot and into a controlled lope around the yard, circling Sandy's car, showing the magnificent Arab at his smooth and elegant best.

"What's that boy doing on that horse?" Paddy Kane's voice exploded across the yard. Forgetting that he was holding the car door open for his injured son, he strode to remonstrate with Hadley, who had just come out of the tack room. "You see what that stupid kid you employ as a so-called wrangler has done now?" he challenged. "He's let another guest up in the saddle of that darned horse!"

Hadley narrowed his eyes and took in Troy and Johnny Mohawk's circular path. Troy was changing rein, altering his commands so that Johnny side-stepped neatly in full view of his growing audience. The horse executed his piece of fancy footwork with perfect ease, tossed his head, and pranced as if he was glad to be back where he belonged—center stage and performing to loud cheers.

"Great!" The Holgate girls called and clapped. "Do it again, Troy!"

"You see that?" By now, Paddy Kane's face was dark red with anger. He pointed in Charlie's direction. "Yesterday he leads a trek and lets a young rider who happens to be my son and who doesn't know the territory go off alone! Today he ignores an order not to let a dangerous horse be ridden!"

"Now, just a minute..." Hadley rose to Charlie's defense, but Kane cut in again.

"It's true! I heard it with my own ears; Mrs. Scott specifically told him that the black horse wasn't to be tacked up. Word for word. 'Charlie, don't let anyone ride Johnny until I've decided what we ought to do about him'!"

As Paddy Kane yelled, Kirstie's mom came around to hold the door while Stevie stepped out of the car.

"It's OK, it was a mistake," Hadley tried to explain. "Troy's a little overenthusiastic, that's all."

"It's not OK!" Kane stormed on and waved his arms in his growing rage. "This horse is the crazy brute that bucked my son off and broke his arm yesterday!"

"Troy can handle him!" Brad Jensen called across the yard, thinking he was helping matters but really making them worse. He pointed to his kid brother trotting Johnny smartly over the wooden bridge into the meadow.

"So could my boy, Stevie!" Enraged by the implied comparison, Paddy Kane turned up the volume. "But if a horse is mean, it doesn't matter how good the rider is. He'll have you off his back and trample all over you without a second thought!"

"We'll make sure Johnny's kept off work for a day or two," Sandy assured him, taking over from Hadley, who had grimaced and turned away. "That'll give us time to check his feet, have Glen Woodford, the vet, take a look at him to see if there's any physical cause for his behavior yesterday..."

Kane shook his head. "Not good enough! If you put this horse back on the trails by the end of this week—in fact, if you decide to use him ever again— it's my opinion that you'll be putting the safety of guests in severe danger!"

Kirstie saw her mom frown and hang her head. She felt her own mouth go dry as she predicted what was coming.

"You want me to take Johnny out of the remuda for good?" Sandy said quietly, standing hands on hips in the middle of the bright yard.

"I know what I'm talking about! I have a trekking center of my own, remember, and thirty years of experience to back me!" Paddy Kane was laying down the law, leaving no one in any doubt. "I'm telling you that horse may look great, but his temperament is suspect. A horse like that is, and always will be, a danger to any rider, however good!"

"Mom, you don't have to listen..." Kirstie began. But Hadley stepped in front of her, shaking his head.

"Later," he cautioned.

"If I see this lousy wrangler out in charge of another group..." Kane worked himself up to a final declaration, ignoring Stevie and pointing the finger of blame wherever he could, "... and if I see or hear of Johnny Mohawk being used on this ranch ever again, I'll do what I said I'd do yesterday; and I'll see you in court!"

* * *

"He means it," Hadley said. "And he believes he's right. The man's pride is at stake."

Sandy, Matt, and Kirstie had gathered in the ranch-house kitchen for a meeting with Hadley and Charlie before the start of the Tuesday morning ride.

"If he recognizes that Troy can handle Johnny Mohawk better than his own son, he loses face. No way can he afford to do that." The old wrangler's gravelly voice confirmed what they all already knew.

Looking around the group of worried faces, Charlie broke the silence. "I'll quit!" he offered. "If it helps, I'll pack my bag and leave!"

"That wouldn't be right!" Kirstie gasped and shook her head. Charlie had just volunteered to sacrifice everything for them.

"No," Sandy and Matt agreed together.

"Anyhow, I doubt that it'd help," Matt put in quietly.

"But the guy blames me." Charlie was in earnest, gripping the brim of his hat with clenched fists. His confidence was obviously low and his conscience was beginning to trouble him. "Some might say he was right."

"We don't say so, Charlie," Sandy replied calmly. "And we're the ones who count around here."

"Looks like you're staying." Hadley gave a satisfied grunt.

"And it looks like Kane will sue." Matt faced facts.

"Maybe." Sandy sighed as she looked out of the window and up the hill to the Kanes' cabin, where Stevie sat on the front porch, a lonely figure nursing his injured arm, while every other guest on the ranch prepared to ride. "Maybe not, if I go halfway to meet him."

"No, Mom, you can't!" This meant a decision about Johnny Mohawk, and Kirstie leaped in to defend him.

"Can't what?" Lisa hovered on the outside of the meeting, not part of it, but unable to help overhearing from where she stood on the landing at the top of the stairs.

"You can't get rid of Johnny. He doesn't deserve it!" Kirstie stood across the doorway as if she would physically stop her mother.

"I said to meet Mr. Kane halfway, not the whole hog." Sandy looked her steadily in the eye. She raised her hat and put it squarely on her blonde head.

"By doing what?" The gaze made Kirstie step to one side and lower her voice.

"By agreeing to take Johnny out of the remuda for the rest of the week," her mom told her. "And I'm gonna tell Mr. Kane that we'll make a final decision on the horse's future no later than the coming weekend!"

6

"Once, when Half Moon was still a cattle ranch and your grandpa ran the place, we had something like this happen," Hadley told Kirstie. He delved back into the history of the ranch to help her understand why Sandy had given in to Paddy Kane's demands.

At first, she was only half-listening, more interested in watching Johnny Mohawk gallop the length of the long, white fence of Red Fox Meadow. The black stallion seemed not to know why he was being left out of the morning ride. The sidelining didn't suit him; he wanted to be out in the corral with the rest of the horses, up front as usual when the wranglers set off along the trails.

Hadley told her the story anyhow as they waited for Matt to head the group of beginners off first. "We had a guy over from Oklahoma to work the spring roundup with us. It was his first time in Colorado, but he came with a big reputation in the professional rodeo events in Oklahoma City: champion calf-roper, champion steer-wrestler. According to him, he'd made a 4.5-second check with a 220-pound steer to clinch the title the previous year. Your grandpa took him at his word, gave him the best horse on the ranch to work with."

"And?" Kirstie grew more interested as she made the comparison with the boasts of Paddy and Stevie Kane.

"And, the first time I rode out to Hummingbird Rock with him to bring back half a dozen steers, I could see he was pretty good..."

"...But not that good!" *Yeah, exactly the same as the Kanes.*

"You got it. No way was this guy a professional champion. And the same sort of thing happened; he tried too hard, pushed his horse where she didn't want to go, came out of the saddle, blamed the horse."

"You saw it?"

"Every last bit, down to him picking himself up and dusting down his fancy new leather chaps."

That was where the difference came in; no one had seen Stevie Kane's accident. "What did you do?" Kirstie asked.

Hadley shrugged. "I never said a word. I just let him tell your grandpa his whole story about the horse bucking and ask for a different mount next day. I knew that it wouldn't make a bit of difference. Even if he got up on a dozen top-grade quarter horses, he still wouldn't make champion steer-wrestler."

"But why didn't you tell Grandpa what you knew?" To Kirstie, it seemed obvious that the truth should have come out.

"Like I said, the man's pride was at stake. It meant a heck of a lot to him. The rest of that roundup, I rode with the guy, took care of anything he couldn't handle. Together, the two of us did pretty good. By the end of the month, he was doing a whole lot better than when he first came."

"You covered up for him for a whole month?"

"Kinda. Your grandpa knew what was going on without me opening my mouth, though. He just gave me a hard look and let us get on with roping those steers."

"But why?" Kirstie had begun to compare Hadley with Lisa, who, when she examined it, also seemed to be covering up for an imposter's poor riding.

Hadley gave another of his casual, barely notice-able shrugs, then made ready to ride Moose out along Bear Hunt Trail. "I guess I kinda liked the guy," he murmured, pulling down the brim of his hat and heading the Jensen boys out of the corral on an all-day ride.

The ban on guests riding Johnny Mohawk, which Sandy had agreed upon with Paddy Kane, didn't include her, Kirstie decided.

She'd spent all morning and most of the afternoon doing jobs on the ranch, cleaning out the tack room and hosing down the stalls in the stable block. Tonight there would be a sing-along beside the creek. Lanterns would light up an old-fashioned chuck wagon which they used as a small stage for the singers, so Kirstie finished her chores by checking the wicks of the lanterns and sweeping the wagon floor. She'd saved the treat of riding Johnny until the end of the day.

But now, as she stored the broom in the tack room and unhitched a head collar from its hook on the wall, ready to head out to the meadow to find Johnny, she realized she was being watched. She'd heard footsteps crunching across the gravel in the yard then stopping, so she turned to see Stevie Kane, his arm in a white sling, a gauze pad covering the wound on his head. Catching her glance, he hurried on across the lawn in front of the ranch house and up the slope toward his cabin.

"Hey." Annoyed by his sulky reaction, Kirstie muttered a sarcastic greeting under her breath, then carried on. She could see Johnny at the fence, as before, looking out and still wondering why he'd been left behind. "I know; it's tough!" she told him as she drew close. She climbed the fence and quickly fitted the head collar, led him to the gate, and laughed as he nudged impatiently at the catch with his nose. "Hold your horses—oh no, you can't do that; you *are* a horse!"

Johnny nickered and fiddled with the catch.

"Yeah, yeah, just let me get at it, then we can be out of here!" They were through the gate, hurrying toward the corral. Johnny was practically leading her, not the other way around. He trotted as she ran into the corral, right up to the tack-room door.

"We just won the world record for tacking up a horse!" she grinned, fetching bit and bridle, then the heavy saddle. "One and a half minutes from start to finish!"

Johnny stamped his feet and snorted. He snaked his neck and turned his head to look over his shoulder, as if to say, *What's the holdup? Why aren't you in the saddle?*

"OK, I'm there!" She hooked her foot into the stirrup and swung up, had hardly settled before the horse took off at a brisk walk, heading for the bridge. "Hey, we're not following the others on the trail!" Kirstie warned, reining him to the right. "We're gonna work in the round pen."

Sure; anything! Johnny changed course and entered the pen, willing as could be. There was a spring in his step, his fine neck was arched, he was looking all about him, waiting to be worked.

So Kirstie put him through his paces, trying the tricky stuff that Troy Jensen had performed, then working more on her own posting trot. She wanted to perfect it without stirrups, but this meant strengthening her thigh muscles, and she knew it wouldn't come right away. She also realized that her balance had to be 100 percent. Sensing her try out something new, Johnny Mohawk continued around the pen at a smooth, steady pace, head up, ears flicked toward his rider, catching Kirstie's every move.

"Great!" Breathless and aching, she sat in the saddle at last. "Good boy, Johnny! You were fantastic!"

The lavish praise must have carried out of the round pen into the yard, because suddenly Lisa's wavy red hair and freckled face appeared over the top of the fence. "Hey, Kirstie, what do you think you're doing?"

"Riding Johnny Mohawk," she said, calmly stating the obvious. Behind Lisa, she caught a glimpse of Stevie Kane hanging around in the yard.

"I can see that. I mean, why? Isn't he supposed to be banned or something?"

"Only from being ridden by dudes." Kirstie intended Stevie to overhear this. "I know Johnny like the back of my hand; I don't find him to be any kind of problem!"

Lisa frowned. "You can never be sure," she warned. "Once a horse has bucked someone off, he gets a mean streak. A horse like that is dangerous."

"Not Johnny!" Kirstie insisted. *Stevie Kane, you'd better hear this!* In the background, she saw the boy slouch off across the lawn. "Look at him; Johnny Mohawk is a fantastic horse!"

"No!" In spite of seeing him behaving like an angel, responding once more to Kirstie's complicated commands, Lisa's surge of sympathy for Stevie made her resist her old friend, Kirstie.

Kirstie trotted him right up to the fence, stopped him in an instant. "Yes!" she argued. Never mind that Stevie Kane had slunk off out of sight, this one was for Lisa: "If you're a halfway decent rider, Johnny is the best, the most perfect horse you could wish for!"

* * *

"In the mornin', I was ridin',
Through the breaks of that wide plain,
With the saddle-leather creakin',
In the sun and in the rain!"

Charlie sang a favorite cowboy song, long legs hanging over the side of the chuck wagon, cropped dark head bent forward over his old guitar.

Tuesday evening, and everyone had gathered around a campfire by the creek. After an open-air supper of barbecued chicken, and with fleece jackets zipped up against a chilly wind, they happily joined in the sing-along.

"Late at night, we were returnin',
Horsemen ridin' wild and free,
Waitin' for the next day's dawnin',
'Cross wide plains, my horse and me!"

Hadley sang the second verse, then sucked and blew on his silver harmonica. He invited the Half Moon guests to join in the chorus.

"That land was ours, that land was free;
Mountains, lakes for all to see!"

Kirstie sang with the rest, but her heart wasn't in it. The disagreement with Lisa that afternoon had left her feeling down—and the fact that Lisa had ignored her ever since. She was sitting now with Stevie Kane on a bench by the fire, light from the flames flickering red and yellow on their faces as they talked. Their expressions were intense, as if whatever they were talking about took up every scrap of their attention, as if the world of the campfire and the people gathered to sing simply didn't exist.

"Anyone would think Lisa didn't have a home to go to," Matt remarked with a grin as he passed Kirstie on his way for a second helping of chicken.

"Hmm." She turned her back on Lisa and Stevie, showing she couldn't care less.

"Uh-oh!" Matt raised his eyebrows. Then his jokey manner changed as he saw Paddy Kane heading for the barbecue, too. "I'm outta here!" he said, quickly changing his mind.

"Good food!" the temperamental Irishman told Sandy Scott, seeming for the time being to have dropped his threat to sue the ranch. His voice carried above a quiet section of harmonica playing from Hadley. "My compliments to the chef!"

From behind the barbecue table, Kirstie's mom thanked him pleasantly.

Yuck! Kirstie couldn't understand why she was being so nice. The guy was smooth and smarmy beyond belief in his riding pants and padded jacket, his hair slicked back after a shower, a false smile on his face.

"Hey, Sandy!" It was Troy Jensen's turn to ask for seconds. Piling potato salad onto his plate, he blundered into a conversation with the Irish visitor. "Say, Mr. Kane, I had me a good idea earlier!"

"Really?" The response was stiff and brief.

"Yeah. Brad and me had this talk about the black stallion: y'know, Johnny Mohawk!"

"I know who you mean." More distance as Kane frowned and took a step back.

Kirstie, on the other hand, got up from her seat and went closer.

"We heard Sandy had cut him out of the remuda," Troy charged on, regardless. "Something about the horse bein' too mean to be ridden?"

"Quite right." Snappy now, and with a deep frown, then a quick glance in Stevie's direction.

"See here, Brad and me don't think that's right. Both me and my brother would love to ride that little black horse for the rest of the week."

Sandy shook her head. "Not possible, Troy. I promised Mr. Kane I'd get the vet to look at him, keep him out of action at least until the weekend."

Kirstie swallowed the urge to tell her mom that she'd ridden Johnny Mohawk that very afternoon and that he'd behaved like an angel. She saw that Stevie and Lisa had looked up from their deep conversation.

"But hey!" Troy protested. He turned to Paddy Kane with a direct challenge. "I got me a better idea."

"Let us in on it, why don't you?" Kane sneered.

"Forget the vet. Let me give Johnny a test."

"No, Troy…" Sandy began.

But Mr. Kane cut in, his face looking shadowy and strange in the flickering light of the log fire. "Hear him out. I'd be interested in what sort of test Troy could invent to prove that the horse is fit to ride!"

91

The Texan boy shrugged. "Easy. I saddle him up and ride him hard on Eagle's Peak Trail. I ask him to cross streams and climb high; all the tough stuff. See if he cracks under pressure."

"No, not possible," Sandy said again. Over on the chuck wagon, the last song of the evening had finished and Charlie had put down his guitar.

But Paddy Kane had narrowed his eyes as he listened. He cleared his throat and passed a hand across his mouth. "You'd never manage to handle the horse on that trail," he said, nervous and uncertain about what to do now that the music had stopped and people were watching and judging. "It's where Stevie had his accident."

"Sure I will!" Troy was casual, laid back, and obviously infuriating to the uptight Irishman. "Try me!"

Kane rubbed his face, coughed, then nodded. Unable to turn down the challenge without losing face, he was forced to agree. "OK, fine. You're on!"

"Yee-hah!" The Texan boy slapped his leg. "I get to ride Johnny Mohawk!" he yelled to his brother.

"B-but..." Sandy Scott was doubtful. She was definitely finding the unpredictable visitor hard to handle. "You sure you don't want to change your mind?" she checked with Paddy Kane.

Attempting a grin that didn't quite work, he shook hands on the deal with a jubilant Troy. "I was never one to turn down a challenge," he said weakly. "I'd lay money on the stallion bucking the boy off before they get out of the valley!"

"You're certain you want to do this?" Sandy still couldn't believe the sudden switch.

"Quite sure. We Irish are great gamblers when it comes to the horses."

Fake, fake, fake! Kirstie breathed.

"And if I ride the horse hard as I can and stay on him, I can have him for the rest of the week?" Troy checked with the ranch boss.

Yes! Kirstie hoped her mom could read her mind. She edged in as close as she could get, eyes wide, holding her breath.

"That would be part of the deal," Paddy Kane acknowledged. His mouth twitched slightly, but there was no turning back. They arranged a time to set off—Hadley leading the ride, Troy on Johnny Mohawk, Paddy Kane going along on Silver Flash as a witness.

"Neat! I know you can do it!" Kirstie flashed Troy a confident smile as the group broke up and people drifted away from the campfire, heading for their cabins and an early night. She turned to Hadley, who was kicking soil over the dying flames. "But why?" she demanded.

"Huh?" The old wrangler killed the last embers with the toe of his boot.

"All that stuff about Kane being ready to accept a challenge wasn't right, was it? I mean, why did he really agree? He must know deep down that Stevie isn't such a great rider and realize that he could lose this bet real easy!"

"He knows it," Hadley agreed. The fire was out; they were in pitch darkness out by Five Mile Creek. The swift water ran noisily between steep banks. "But pride's a funny thing. Pride leads you places you don't want to go. It sets you up for a great big fall!"

7

Deep down, Kirstie didn't care. All this complicated stuff about Stevie's mom dying and his dad's weird desire to save face wasn't nearly so important to her as proving that Johnny Mohawk was one of the best horses at Half Moon Ranch.

"Today's the day!" she told Lisa as she leaped out of bed and into her riding clothes of jeans, boots, and T-shirt. She determinedly ignored the fact that her friend had come inside after the sing-along and gone to bed without a single word.

The hump inside the blue sleeping bag in the corner made no sound.

Not asleep, but still not talking! Kirstie had already heard Lisa turn restlessly from side to side in the predawn light. Hurt as she was by her friend's sudden switch of allegiance, she decided the best thing to do was pretend she didn't care.

She left Lisa to stew and ran down the stairs two at a time. The hall clock said five thirty, way too early for anyone else to be up, and two and a half hours until Troy, Paddy Kane, and Hadley were due to set out. Two and a half restless hours, during which she was too excited and nervous to eat breakfast, too impatient to stay in the house.

So Kirstie pulled her baseball cap from its hook by the door and slipped outside into the cool, misty morning. She startled a chipmunk scouting for tidbits under the porch swing. The tiny creature saw her, swiped his striped tail from side to side, chattered, and scuttled off across the boards.

Now was the time to see wildlife, as the sun rose over Hummingbird Rock to slowly warm the wet, dark shadows beneath rocks and trees and to drive danger from the landscape. Searching the hillside beyond the creek, she counted three mule deer with their long, tapering antlers and large, mule-like ears. Closer to home, she saw a gray fox creep from the cover of a log pile outside the Kanes' cabin and slink off into the trees.

Something had disturbed the fox, she realized. Despite the early hour, she wasn't surprised to see the cabin door open and Stevie Kane peer out. What did surprise her was the way he acted next: creeping out across the porch as sly and silent as the old fox, looking this way and that as he crossed the lawn and headed for the corral.

Quickly, Kirstie stepped out of sight behind a rain barrel close to the house. She felt like a fool for hiding; it was like she was a little kid. But something told her not to let Stevie know she was there. Crouching behind the barrel, she watched him enter and cross the corral, then vanish inside the tack room.

She waited a few seconds while she decided what to do. What was he up to in there at this time of the morning? Why had he been so keen not to be seen? A gut feeling told her that the reasons were connected with Johnny Mohawk. *Yeah!* she told herself. *You get in there and find out exactly what he's doing.*

So she did some creeping of her own. Across the yard, treading softly, heading for fresh cover on the porch around the back of the tack room, she reached a window and peered inside. At first, she saw no sign of Stevie, only the glint of bridles hanging on the wooden walls and the soft shine of saddles slung across their stout racks down the middle of the room. Then hollow footsteps; Stevie Kane turned a corner and came along the row of saddles toward her, carefully reading the labels tacked to the wall. Lucky, Cadillac, Crazy Horse, Yukon... Johnny Mohawk. He stopped suddenly, took a quick look over his shoulder, then delved deep into his jacket pocket.

Time to leave the window and circle around to the door, Kirstie decided. Soft as a cat, hardly daring to breathe, she edged along the porch. She shouldn't have worried; when she reached the open doorway and finally dared to poke her head around the doorpost, Stevie was too busy with Johnny's saddle to notice her.

She watched him with a puzzled frown. Whatever

he'd taken from his pocket was small and needed to be handled carefully. He placed it gingerly on top of the saddle, then lifted the flap, felt with his good, left hand in the gap between the stirrup leather and the pad of thick fabric called the comforter—a kind of small rug used to stop the saddle rubbing the horse's back. As soon as he found a suitable space, he took the object from the top of the saddle and slipped it inside.

"No way!" Kirstie's heart was in her mouth as she stepped suddenly into the room.

Stevie let the saddle flap fall into position, then spun around. "What?" He put on an innocent face. "Kirstie! You gave me a fright coming in like that!"

She ignored him. "Don't give me that. Just show me what you put under Johnny's saddle!"

"I don't know what you mean!"

Wounded innocence now; all fake, just like his father. Kirstie pushed past him and felt along the stirrup leather until her fingers came up against something sharp. "Ouch!" She drew her hand back and sucked the spot of blood that had appeared. Then carefully, slowly, she tried again. This time, she was able to pull out the object and hold it up. "Razor wire!"

"Don't look at me! I didn't know it was there!" White in the face, shaking all over, Stevie jumped to deny it.

Kirstie gasped and turned on him. She walked right up to him, shoved the dangerous, two-inch stretch of wire under his nose. "You know the damage this could do? It could cut deep!" Shock, then scorn, filled her voice as she realized what Stevie was up to. "... You were trying to set Johnny up!"

"I don't know what you're talking about!" He stood his ground. A blank, hard look came into his eyes.

"This!" She held the razor wire closer still.

"I've never seen it before."

"Liar!" Kirstie's hand began to shake. If Stevie denied it, it would be difficult to make people believe her, she knew. There were no witnesses. It would sound too cruel, too crazy to suggest.

"I... never... saw... it!" Stevie's eyes were dead, the pupils big and dark.

"All to prove you're right!" Kirstie cried. "A trick to get Troy bucked off and Johnny Mohawk proved guilty! Then what? Johnny gets banned. Mom can't use him on the ranch without your dad taking us to court and suing us for every cent we've got! Worse than that—if we can't use Johnny, what do we do with him? We can't afford to keep him if he can't work. So what happens to him then?"

"You sell him," Stevie said, cold as ice, the words of a much younger kid creeping in. "And good riddance to bad rubbish!"

But the plan had backfired, and there was no razor

wire to rub through the blanket and dig into Johnny's skin as Troy rode him out along Eagle's Peak Trail.

Instead, Troy and Johnny Mohawk made a dream team, and Kirstie was there to see it happen.

"Sure; come along," Hadley had told her when she asked if she could join the group. A rush of feelings—anger mixed with fear, confusion and concern for Lisa—had forced Kirstie to stay silent about the incident with Stevie Kane in the tack room, but she'd made doubly sure to check all Johnny's tack before Troy got up in the saddle, examining the cinch strap and stirrups, as well as the comforter. Relying on Troy's skill to bring Johnny the reprieve she longed for, she'd watched him mount with quiet confidence. Then she'd thrown Stevie a withering look as his dad had set off on Cadillac. The look had said, *I'll get you!* And now she muttered aloud, "Everyone's been feeling sorry for you until now. But I'll prove you've been lying all along!"

Stevie had turned his back, head down, shoulders hunched with worry.

Kirstie and Lucky were keeping pace with Troy and Johnny Mohawk up the trail, through the lodgepole pines to where the trees thinned out and patches of snow began. The horses' hooves crunched through the pure white drifts, the sky grew dense blue, a breeze rippled through a stretch of alpine forget-me-nots.

"It's looking good!" Troy called as he went ahead. "Johnny's on his best behavior! He's out of this world!"

Kirstie nodded. The stallion's jet-black coat gleamed in the sunlight, he went surefooted along the narrow ridge by the pointed rock. "This is where Stevie had the accident!" she reminded Troy.

Paddy Kane also recognized the spot. He held Cadillac back, refusing at first to take him along the ridge.

"There's something he's not telling us!" Kirstie murmured. She'd learned to second guess the Kanes' reasons for doing or not doing things. "Go steady, Troy!" she called. "Just in case!"

"Sure thing!" The Texan kid slowed Johnny's pace as he rounded the bend and the track narrowed right down to single file. The rider was relaxed, the horse listening to commands.

"Walk on, Lucky!" Kirstie urged. The palomino

had hesitated, his eyes and ears alert. "What's he telling us?" she asked Hadley, who had ridden up close behind.

The wrangler shrugged. "Look, listen. Trust your horse."

By this time, Troy and Johnny were out of sight, so Kirstie pressed Lucky forward, taking the bend at a trot. She saw Johnny pause by the rock where Stevie had waited all afternoon for help, admiring the way Troy handled him gently but firmly to get him past a spot he obviously didn't like. The horse tossed his head for a moment, then lowered it and carried on, picking up the pace again as he reached the far end of the ridge.

"Nothing to it!" Troy turned and yelled for them all to follow.

Kirstie and Lucky kept on going. As the track narrowed and fell away steeply, she spotted the churned up ground where Johnny had thrown his rider. Then a few steps beyond this, Lucky suddenly stopped.

What was it? Kirstie looked up and down the slope. Three trees had fallen a few yards higher up and formed a crisscross pattern with their trunks.

Brushwood blown by the strong winds had collected against them in a thick tangle of branches and briars. But there seemed to be a tunnel through the brushwood, deep under the fallen trunks, to a place offering shelter and safety to an animal, perhaps. Kirstie saw that it must be a large animal whose claws had scratched and torn at the entrance to the tunnel, scraping away earth and piling it to either side.

"Bears!" Hadley murmured.

Kirstie froze in her saddle. "That's their den?"

The old man nodded. "It looks like a bed site for the mother bear and her two cubs. She banks up the soil for extra heat."

She scanned the hillside anxiously, expecting to see a bulky creature with a large, square head, huge shoulders, and long claws lumber out of the forest toward them. From what she knew about black bears, it could come at them at a speed of 30 miles per hour, and nothing, but nothing, would stop a mother bear if you came between her and her cubs.

"Let's get out of here," Hadley suggested, calling Paddy Kane to join them from behind. "The bears are most probably out foraging up the mountain at this time of day and they won't be back before nightfall, but it's not a good idea to hang around."

Kirstie was only too glad to oblige. She pressed a reluctant Lucky on, holding him on a tight rein until they came off the ridge. "Did you see the bear's den?" She gasped out the news to Troy.

"Where? Wow, that's really wild!" He followed the line of her pointing finger. "Do you reckon that's maybe what bothered Johnny the first time Stevie brought him along here?"

Watching Hadley backtrack to try and persuade Paddy Kane to bring Cadillac along the ridge, Kirstie nodded. "Bears!" she whispered.

"Kirstie, Troy!" Hadley called from the tower of rock. "Paddy doesn't want to risk the ridge with Cadillac!"

"I bet he doesn't!" she breathed. "I bet he's known about the den since Monday!" Stevie's father had been the one who'd walked the track looking for clues. It was her guess that he'd spotted the brushwood den then, guessed that it housed some pretty big animal, but said nothing.

"We'll go back down the way we came!" Hadley called. "You two go right ahead. We'll see you back at the ranch!"

"…He's chicken and he's a liar!" Kirstie told Troy all she knew about Paddy Kane as they rode down the mountain together. "He guessed the bear's den had spooked Johnny, and Stevie hadn't been able to handle it. But he kept it secret and blamed the horse."

"But we showed him!" Troy let Johnny Mohawk lengthen his stride as they came out of the aspen trees into the sun. There was half a mile of good loping ground between them and the ranch. "We made a deal, and we showed him what Johnny can really do. He's a great horse, and now I get to ride him between now and Saturday!"

Once before during this week, Kirstie had put Lucky into a race against Johnny and won. But today was different. She saw the black Arab horse surge along the riverbank, watched him swerve to avoid a rock and gallop on. He was full of himself, enjoying his speed, lost in his own strength and perfection.

No contest! Not with Johnny Mohawk in this

mood. Not with a natural horseman like Troy in the saddle. She sighed happily and let Lucky lope for home a lazy second.

"Too late, I'm afraid!" Paddy Kane pretended to be sorry. It was Thursday morning, and the postman had just delivered the mail to the ranch.

Sandy Scott held an attorney's letter in her trembling hand. "But we had a deal!" she insisted. "If Troy could handle Johnny Mohawk without any problem, you promised not to make any more trouble!"

Kirstie felt her throat hurt as she swallowed. It was anger rising up from her stomach, making her want to yell that this wasn't fair.

"But the letter was already on its way, you see." The Irishman made out that the important fact had slipped his mind. "I'd set the whole thing in motion the day before yesterday. So the fluke circumstance of Troy getting back in one piece doesn't make any difference. Once the lawyers get their teeth into something, you know what they're like!"

"It says here you plan to sue us for personal injury!" Sandy read the letter through as Matt and Kirstie stood nearby. They'd all come up to the

Kanes' cabin as soon as they'd taken in what had happened.

"You lied to us!" Matt shook his head in disgust, ready to drive Sandy straight into San Luis to visit their own attorney.

"My hands are tied. Sorry."

"You could still call off the lawyers, keep your word." Matt's tone of voice showed that he knew it was a forlorn hope.

Kane spread his hands helplessly. "I'm offering you a clear way out of all this, and it's in the last paragraph of the letter, if you care to read it."

Sandy opened the sheet of paper and spoke the words out loud. "'As the owner of his own trekking center in Ireland, my client's whole concern is for the future safety of guest riders at Half Moon Ranch. Accordingly, we would inform you that he is prepared to drop all claims for damages against you and your employee, Charlie Miller, on one particular condition.'" Glancing up at Kirstie, Sandy took a breath, then read on. "'Namely that the horse involved in the incident, Johnny Mohawk, is never used as a trail horse or in any other capacity whatsoever; that the said horse is taken to a sale barn and sold, and thus that no guest is put into the position of risk to life and limb that his son, Stevie Kane, endured on Monday, 2nd July. Yours, et cetera…'"

"Meaning we have no choice!" Matt insisted. The car engine was running, Sandy was in the house, calling to tell the attorney that she and Matt were on their way.

"Meaning we have to sell Johnny Mohawk because Stevie Kane is a liar and his dad is a lousy cheat!" Hot tears sprang to Kirstie's eyes.

"Meaning this whole thing is out of control," Sandy said quietly as she crossed the porch and got into the car. "A court case, insurance claims, bad publicity: I tell you, I don't need it!"

"Look at him now!" Kirstie couldn't be calm like her mom. She waved her arm toward the corral, at Stevie Kane acting tough with the Jensen brothers, all three of them cracking up over some stupid joke. Rodeo Rocky and Jitterbug stood quietly nearby, while Linda and Carole Holgate leaned on the fence to watch. "Why does he have to show off like that after all the trouble he's caused?"

Sandy sighed at what was going on. "Sorry, honey, we have to go. If they start fooling around in there, find Hadley. He'll have to deal with it."

Kirstie glowered and fell silent. She hated the sight of the kid and his greasy, double-crossing father. Now, instead of watching Stevie laugh and swagger in front of the girls, she turned her back.

As Matt drove her mom up the drive, she planned to keep on ignoring the boys' hoarse laughs and yells from the corral. But then one of the girls let out a shriek.

"Hey, Stevie, no!" Carole Holgate cried.

Kirstie swung around to look. "Oh my gosh!" She double-checked. Brad had already jumped onto Jitterbug, and now Stevie was struggling one-handed into Rocky's saddle. She set off at a run toward the corral. In spite of everything, she had to try and stop the crazy fool.

"Stevie, don't do that!" she yelled.

He was mounted and walking the horse toward the gate, following close in Brad and Jitterbug's tracks. He was deliberately ignoring her.

Slamming up against the fence in her desperate

hurry, Kirstie winded herself. "Stop!" she gasped. Her heart practically stopped beating from fear and panic. "Stevie, for goodness sake, come back before you kill yourself!"

8

"...Look, I can ride one-handed. It's easy!" Stevie ignored Kirstie's cries. He held Rodeo Rocky's reins in his left hand. His broken arm was heavily bandaged and kept in a crooked position by a strong hospital sling.

"Stevie, don't be a fool!" Carole Holgate echoed Kirstie's warnings.

Seeing that it was useless, Kirstie ran into the tack room, then straight back out. "Has anybody seen

Hadley or Charlie?" she demanded, recalling her mom's advice before she'd set off for town for her emergency meeting with the attorney.

"Hadley already set off with the intermediates," Linda told her. "The Jensens decided to take the morning off and maybe go fishing. And Charlie went to town. It's his day off. That's why Rodeo Rocky was hanging around for Stevie to climb on."

"Look at this!" Stevie steered Rocky past Brad through the corral gate, weaving between two posts in a neat and tricky maneuver.

"That's nothin'!" The older Jensen brother took up the challenge by dropping Jitterbug's reins. He rode her out onto the footbridge using only his legs and heels.

"Why can't they grow up?" Kirstie muttered. With both wranglers off the scene, it was up to her to put a stop to the stupid competition. And she had to contend with the strong thought that if Stevie fell off again, it would serve him right. Glowering, and aware now that Troy Jensen was leading a horse out of the barn to join in the so-called fun, she set off on foot for the bridge.

"I can trot, no problem!" Stevie cried, sitting

awkwardly because of his injured arm. Rocky crossed the bridge at a gentle trot, probably aware that his rider wasn't safe and easy in the saddle.

"Not a good idea, Stevie!" Kirstie called.

"Hey, who said?" Brad grinned down at her. He urged his dainty sorrel horse after Rodeo Rocky, yee-hahing as he raced to catch up. "How about a lope?" he yelled at Stevie, who swayed as he turned to see who was following.

Kirstie closed her eyes and groaned. She opened them again as Troy trotted by. "Oh, no!" If she'd thought things couldn't get any worse, she'd been wrong. Hotheaded Troy was riding Johnny Mohawk to join the others. "Come back!" she pleaded. "Troy, you can't use Johnny today. No one can!"

"Yeah, yeah! I won the bet, didn't I?" He was going from trot to lope, giving Johnny his head. The black Arab's tail streamed out behind him, his hooves ate up the ground.

"Hey, Troy!" Brad reined Jitterbug back to wait for his kid brother. Up ahead, Stevie took Rocky in a wide arc, up a gentle slope and back toward Troy and Brad.

"You wanna race?" Troy challenged.

Brad quickly agreed. "You and me. The first to reach Dead Man's Canyon."

"How about you, Stevie?" Troy asked as Kirstie sprinted to try and stop them. Johnny Mohawk was tossing his handsome head and snorting impatiently.

"Count me in," Stevie answered, fake-casual. But a catch in his voice showed he was scared. "Dead Man's Canyon; that's the Meltwater Trail?"

"Yup. Along Five Mile Creek, cut up toward Miners' Ridge, head through Fat Man's Squeeze into the canyon." Brad issued directions then added, "We'll give you a couple of minutes' start because of your arm."

Stevie frowned. "I don't need any favors. I want a fair race."

"Listen, no one's racing anywhere!" Kirstie gasped as she drew close. Her face was hot, her heart thumping. "For a start, Troy, we're in real trouble if Mom finds out you saddled Johnny Mohawk. We've got to put him back in the meadow before she gets home. And second, Stevie, no way should you even be riding!"

"Yes, ma'am, no ma'am!" Troy joggled his head from side to side, laughing off her protest. Johnny

Mohawk stamped hard and wheeled away from the group.

"Brad!" Kirstie appealed to the older boy.

"It's not my problem," he shrugged.

She turned desperately to Stevie, reaching out for Rocky's rein. "This is serious!" she pleaded. "Whatever you do, don't race!"

But he tugged hard at the horse's head, jerking him out of Kirstie's grasp and kicking up dirt as he swung him around. "Since when did you worry about me?"

Dust rose and choked her. "Stevie, I mean it!"

"Save your breath!" He kicked hard with his heels, made Rocky surge forward. "Let's go!" he yelled to Troy and Brad, thrown back in the saddle and struggling for balance.

The Jensens didn't need a second invitation. "Cool it!" Brad grinned at Kirstie in the moments before he followed Stevie and Rocky, as Troy and Johnny Mohawk set off in hot pursuit. "Ain't nothing bad gonna happen, I promise!"

Kirstie had stood helpless, watching the three riders race out of sight between the aspen trees

before she'd come to her senses. Then she'd pulled herself together and run for the ranch house to get help from the only person around.

"Lisa!" She flung open the door and ran into the kitchen. The two girls had hardly spoken for days. Ever since Stevie's accident, Lisa had made it plain she was on his side. She'd even stopped riding the trails with Kirstie, preferring instead to spend time with her new friend.

She appeared now from behind Kirstie, hovering warily in the doorway. "Here I am. I was out on the porch."

"I missed you. Listen, I've got a big, big problem!" she gabbled.

"Stevie on Rodeo Rocky," Lisa interrupted. "I know."

"You saw him out in the corral?"

"Yeah. He was trying to impress Linda and Carole, I guess."

"OK, so riding Rocky around the corral is one thing. Racing the Jensens up to Dead Man's Canyon—that's different!" As she spilled out what had happened, Kirstie saw Lisa's face change. Stiff and suspicious at first, it grew flickery and scared at the idea of a flat-out race up the mountain.

Lisa turned and ran into the yard, turned again to wait for Kirstie. "We gotta do something!"

"Stevie's never gonna make it one-handed!"

"Don't tell me; I know it!" Lisa gazed along the valley toward Miners' Ridge. "He always has to prove something!" she wailed. "And now look!"

"OK." Kirstie saw she would have to take charge. "Here's what we do. Lucky and Cadillac are in the barn waiting for the blacksmith to arrive. We saddle them up fast as we can, and we follow the boys!"

Lisa nodded and ran with her to fetch bridles and saddles. Within minutes, they'd made the two horses ready to ride. "They've got a mighty big start on us, though!"

"But we know where they're headed." Kirstie grew more determined. "We follow Meltwater Trail. Sooner or later, we'll catch up with them. Then you have to talk to Stevie, Lisa; make him see sense!"

"Me?" Lisa swung into the saddle. "You want *me* to persuade him to come back to the ranch?"

"You got it!" Kirstie was up and ready, trotting Lucky out onto the trail. "It stands to reason; Stevie doesn't hear a word anyone else says, but he'll listen to you!"

They rode hard along the side of Five Mile Creek, following its bends, scouring the hills ahead for any sign of the three boys.

"Uh-oh!" Kirstie heard the telltale clink of a loose shoe as Lucky's hooves thudded across gravel and rock. The palomino's gait was uneven, the shoe bothering him as they galloped. "This is why Hadley put him on the list to see the blacksmith, I guess!"

"Wait!" Lisa had continued to keep a lookout

as Kirstie slowed Lucky, down then dismounted to examine the state of his front shoe. "Here come Brad and Troy!"

"What about Stevie?" The shoe had worked completely loose, hanging on by a single nail. Unless Kirstie was very careful, the tender underside of Lucky's foot could easily be damaged.

Standing in the stirrups, Lisa craned to see beyond the two galloping horses. "No, there's no sign of Stevie."

"What now?" Kirstie groaned. Another accident? One more broken limb? She regretted wishing that Rocky would throw Stevie and teach him a lesson.

"What happened?" Lisa yelled above the thud of approaching hooves. "Where's Stevie?"

Troy pulled up in the usual spray of dirt. Even though he'd been in a race, Johnny Mohawk had hardly broken a sweat. "You tell us!" he shrugged.

"You mean you don't know?" Kirstie spread both palms in a frustrated, helpless gesture. She left Lucky's side and stormed over to Brad Jensen. "You get into a race with a one-armed kid who had stitches in a gash on his head less than forty-eight hours back, and you come and tell us you don't know where he is?"

"Hey, hang loose," Brad protested. He jumped down from Jitterbug to give her a breather. "It was like this: the Irish kid said he wanted a fair race, so that's what we gave him. We reach the trees and spread out. I take one way up to Miners' Ridge, Troy takes another way, and we leave it to Stevie to choose his own track, OK?"

"You fanned out across the slope?" Kirstie got it clear in her own mind. "Then what?"

"Me and Jitterbug, we get into a close thing with Troy and Johnny. I guess we forgot about Stevie for a while."

"Johnny made it to the canyon ahead of Jitterbug!" Troy claimed. "He won easy!"

"Not that easy." Brad gave him an argument. "Jitterbug could've come first if she hadn't slipped in Fat Man's Squeeze!"

"Hey, it's Stevie we're talking about here!" Lisa reminded them sharply. "Where did he and Rodeo Rocky get to by the time you were in Dead Man's Canyon?"

"Ah, yeah..." Troy looked at Brad and shook his head.

"Well, I guess we don't know." Brad was equally nonplussed. "We wait a few minutes, expecting him to show."

"But the kid doesn't make it." Troy picked up the thread of the story. "What can we do? We turn around and look for him on the way down."

"How hard?" Lisa demanded. "How hard did you look for Stevie?"

"...He's got a broken arm and stitches in his head," Kirstie reminded them again.

Brad sighed. "We reckoned he'd turned back. Looks like we were wrong."

"So you gave up on him!" Lisa yelled. "Honestly, Brad!"

Kirstie hushed her. "There's no point. We have to think." Looking at a still-fresh Johnny Mohawk, she quickly decided what to do. "Here, Troy, you take Lucky and walk him back to the ranch. His shoe's loose, see? I'll take Johnny. Lisa and me will ride up to the ridge and make sure Stevie and Rocky are OK."

Troy gave her no argument. Instead, he slid out

of the saddle and handed over the reins. "I still think there's no big problem," he said.

"You hope!" Lisa narrowed her eyes and scowled down at him.

"You worry too much, you know that?" Troy threw his shoulders back and his chest out. "Stevie's a big boy. He can take care of himself."

"Sure," Brad agreed. He, too, kept up the bravado as Kirstie and Lisa got ready to ride on. "You only got one thing to watch out for up in Dead Man's Canyon today, and it ain't Stevie Kane."

"What then?" Kirstie wanted to know.

"It's hairy and black with sharp claws!" Troy crowed. "It's mean and it's angry…"

"The bear!" Lisa mumbled, glancing quickly at the mountain.

Kirstie took a deep breath, then nodded. If the Jensens were right and the mother bear really was prowling around the canyon, no way was this funny. "Let's go!" she hissed, turning Johnny Mohawk and racing him toward Miners' Ridge.

9

"I'm scared!" Lisa admitted.

She and Kirstie had galloped through the silvery aspen trees. They'd bushwhacked through pines and crossed tumbling mountain streams without seeing a sign of Stevie and Rodeo Rocky. Hearing their approach, mule deer had leaped clear of bushes and bounded up the slope and far away. Smaller creatures had crept with a rustle and a frightened squeak under the shelter of leaf and log.

"Me, too." It was one of those times when silence was the last thing you wanted. It crowded in on you, made you imagine things you didn't really hear, like the snort of a black bear calling her cubs.

"What was that?" Lisa gasped. They'd come to a point on the trail when they had to choose either to climb onto Miners' Ridge or to take the narrow entrance between steep, gray cliffs into Dead Man's Canyon.

"Nothing," Kirstie insisted. She decided on the canyon. It was possible that Stevie had eventually followed Troy and Brad in there, only to find that they'd already finished the race and decided to head for home. "C'mon, Johnny; easy, boy!" The horse shied away from the entrance, suspicious of the shadowy rocks.

"Here, let me take Cadillac through first," Lisa suggested. The big, white gelding had a steady nerve, unlike the sometimes-jumpy Arab. She eased ahead of Kirstie into the canyon.

Kirstie clicked and urged Johnny on. Reluctantly, he followed, unsettled now by the crash and roar of the waterfall at the far end of the ravine. For a few moments, it was all she could do to hold him.

"This place gives me the creeps!" Lisa muttered as Kirstie brought Johnny back under control and she peered along its length. "I keep imagining things crouched in the shadows..."

At that second, Kirstie saw the bear. She was on her hind legs, and nearly six feet high, standing on a ledge beside the fall. Her mouth was open to show her giant, pointed teeth. "Back out!" Kirstie cried to Lisa, pulling hard on Johnny's reins. "C'mon, Lisa, let's get out of here!"

But it was too late. The bear had seen them. She snorted and swatted the air, lumbered down from the ledge toward them. Frozen with fright, Kirstie spotted two cubs knee-deep in the pool at the foot of the waterfall. Their shaggy coats were dripping wet, and they were play fighting like boxers sparring in a ring. Mother bear protecting her cubs: it was the worst, the very worst thing they could come up against!

"What do we do?" Lisa panicked as the huge bear advanced. She wrenched on Cadillac's reins, making the poor horse rear up in confusion. Slipping sideways, Lisa lurched forward, flung her arms around the horse's neck, and pulled him off balance as she slid to the ground.

Cadillac was down on his knees, struggling free

of Lisa's grasp. She was on all fours, unhurt but terrified, crawling away from the bear. The gap was narrowing, the bear gathering speed and hurtling down the canyon toward her.

Emergency! Kirstie snapped into action. She yelled loudly to attract the angry bear's attention. Crazy, but this was what you had to do: shout and wave your arms, make the bear back off.

Lisa had frozen. She crouched on the ground while Cadillac broke free and raced toward the exit. The bear opened its jaws and roared.

Kirstie shouted louder still. She made Johnny advance across the bear's path, feeling him flinch and resist. If only she could get him to rear up, to tower over the bear and scare her off, she would save Lisa from attack. "C'mon, Johnny!" she breathed, leaning right back and shortening the reins.

The black horse's muscles bunched and tensed. His nostrils flared wide and his ears flattened. The bear kept on coming. Johnny went back on his haunches and raised his front hooves high in the air, whirling and flailing as he screamed a warning for the bear to stop.

Kirstie lurched backward, strove for balance, found it. Her legs gripped the sides of the rearing horse; backward, forward, then back again she swayed as the horse's front legs came up, down, and then up a second time.

The bear saw the dangerous hooves, heard the scream and the mighty thud as Johnny hit the ground. She swerved off course from her angry attack, then slowed to a suspicious prowl, one eye on her cubs, one eye on Johnny Mohawk.

"Help!" Lisa cried faintly. She stretched out her hand.

Kirstie and Johnny lunged forward as the bear hovered at a distance of about twenty feet. Kirstie stooped to grab hold of her friend's hand. "Jump up!" she cried, desperately hoping that Johnny understood what she was asking him to do now.

Lisa used all her strength to hang onto Kirstie's arm and swing herself onto the horse's back. She made it, gasping for breath, clasping Kirstie around the waist as Johnny braced himself for the weight of an extra rider.

"OK?" Kirstie yelled above the roar of the water, her heart thudding. She felt Lisa nod. "Go, Johnny!"

Kicking him into action, she felt him surge away, strong and steady. The exit to the canyon loomed, steep rock to either side, the crash of the waterfall behind.

"Good boy, Johnny!" she breathed, her heart in her mouth as he raced out of Dead Man's Canyon and carried them to safety.

"Gosh, am I glad you remembered what to do!" Lisa let out a long sigh. She was sitting on the ground high above Dead Man's Canyon, waiting for her knees to stop trembling, her heartbeat to return to normal. "I've never been attacked by a bear before!"

"Me, neither," Kirstie confessed, standing between the recently retrieved Cadillac and Johnny Mohawk, searching the ravine for any sign that the bears might be following. "But I do know you should never back off. You have to wave your arms and yell. You start walking toward a bear and she'll most likely run away."

Lisa was still shuddering from the experience. "I'm sure glad you got me out of there. Bears can kill calves and fawns," she reminded Kirstie.

"But they hardly ever come after humans. It was

because we took her by surprise. And I don't blame her. She must have thought we were after her cubs."

"How can anything so cute grow up into something so awesome? Did you see the little guys playing in the pool?" Lisa took a big breath and stood up. "Anyway, thanks, Kirstie!"

"Thank Johnny," she murmured ruefully, thinking she'd heard a rustling in the scrub below, then dismissing the idea. "And you know, we're no nearer to finding Stevie and Rodeo Rocky."

"Don't tell me. What's he gonna do if he comes face to face with Mama Bear?"

"What most people do, I guess, which is turn and run." Kirstie pictured it with growing worry. "We'd better find him before she does. Are you OK to go on?"

"Sure." Lisa took Cadillac's reins from Kirstie, but as she did, they heard a horse's hooves heading down from the top of Miners' Ridge.

"Thank heavens!" Kirstie caught a glimpse of Rodeo Rocky's sorrel coat and black mane through the trees.

"Stevie!" Lisa called, hurrying her horse up the slope.

"He's limping!" Kirstie lost sight of him, but she heard the uneven tread. Then when Rocky came back into view, her heart sank. There was no Stevie; the horse's saddle was empty.

Lisa stopped. "Oh, no!" she whispered, staring and shaking her head.

"Rocky's seen us, he's on his way down to meet us." Instantly, Kirstie realized that the horse was the one who could lead them to Stevie. She told Lisa to mount and get ready, watching the ex–rodeo horse pick his way carefully down the slope, keeping his weight off the left front leg, which was torn and bloody.

Lisa frowned and pointed to the wound. "How did that happen?"

"Who knows? But look, he wants us to follow!" Kirstie saw Rocky dip his head and turn. Without a shadow of a doubt, he was telling them to come with him. He turned again, bad leg eased clear of the ground, waiting.

So Kirstie went ahead of Lisa, fearing the worst. The riderless horse was bad news, but it figured: Stevie must have fallen way behind Troy and Brad in the race, somehow missed the entrance to Dead

Man's Canyon, and allowed Rocky to gallop recklessly up the steep slope onto the ridge. At some point, the horse had stumbled and hurt his leg. The fall had thrown the boy, who hadn't been able to stay in the saddle because of his broken arm. *Crazy!* she said savagely to herself. This went way beyond the limits of showing off, or "saving face," as Hadley called it. This was craziness, pure and simple.

"What if Stevie's dead?" Lisa half-gasped, half-sobbed. The scare in the ravine had wrecked her nerve, and now the sight of Rocky toiling up the hill, limping and bleeding, set her trembling all over again.

Kirstie gritted her teeth and shook her head. "Don't even think it!" She worked Johnny hard to catch up with Rocky, dreading what they might find behind each boulder, beyond each twist and bend in the sorrel horse's difficult path.

At last, they reached the top of the ridge. The pine trees which grew thickly on the slope thinned out. Ahead were two massive humps of earth and rubble which Kirstie recognized as waste from old mine workings. The bare heaps had grassed over during the decades that had passed since the miners had abandoned the old silver mine. Now wild roses grew and bloomed, their pale pink flowers dappled by sunlight and shade.

Rocky had paused on the ridge, then limped on. He passed the waste heaps and drew level with an arched entrance blasted into the rock. The entrance was shut off by a crumbling wooden door where the sorrel horse stopped.

"It's the way into the mine!" Lisa whispered. "But where's Stevie? I can't see him!"

Kirstie stared hard. There was a pile of brushwood against the door and scraped earth—telltale signs of a second den site. Another picture formed inside her head of Stevie falling from his horse by the mine entrance and coming face to face with the bears in their den, the mother surprised by the sudden intrusion, lumbering out of the entrance toward the injured boy..."No!" she whispered. The rest was too bad to imagine.

"Stevie!" In her panic, Lisa had begun to shout. "Say something! Where are you?"

"Some... thing... are you?" Her voice bounced off the wall of the ravine and echoed back at them.

Down below, there was a small, scratchy sound, then the *chuff-chuff-snort* of a wary black bear still prowling along the near side of the canyon. Looking more closely, Kirstie spotted the cubs scrambling up the slope, tumbling over logs, rolling and picking themselves up.

Lisa flung herself from Cadillac's back and ran for the mine entrance. She rushed past Rodeo Rocky, pushing aside thorn bushes and brushwood close to the entrance. "I still can't see him!" she cried to Kirstie.

"Shh! Listen!" She cocked her head toward the archway of blasted rock beyond the stack of brushwood. The rotting door led to a tunnel that burrowed deep into the mountain with shafts leading off to the left and right: the miners' warren that had once held a bright, gleaming promise of fabulous wealth—and danger. Men had died in the scramble for silver. Rockfalls and floods had put an end to their dreams.

"Here!" a faint voice called out. "Lisa, I'm in here!"

"Stevie?" Lisa spun around toward the door as Kirstie slipped from the saddle and quickly tethered both horses to a tree.

"Go ahead. I'll watch for the bears!" She went to crouch at the edge of the ridge, picking out the three black shapes as they made their way up the rocky slope.

"I'm trapped. I can't get out!" Stevie's voice was muffled, cracked with fear.

"Are you OK?" Wading through the brushwood, pushing it to one side, Lisa began to shove against the door.

"Yeah. There are bears out there. Watch out!"

"I know. We saw them. Kirstie's here with me. She's keeping a lookout! What happened?"

"Rocky wouldn't go into the canyon. I guess he knew about the bears. He got spooked and loped onto the ridge. With my arm in this sling, I couldn't handle him..." Stevie's voice trailed off.

Lisa pushed harder against the door. "It's OK, tell me the rest later. The important thing is to get you out. How come this is jammed?"

"Get a move on!" Kirstie pleaded. She decided not to tell Lisa and Stevie how close the bears were to the ridge. But she backed away from the edge, hoping that they couldn't see or hear the activity outside the entrance to their summer den.

"Rocks!" Stevie explained. "When I saw the bear coming at me over those waste heaps, I saw the door was hanging open and climbed in here to hide. But when I slammed the door shut, I loosened a whole lot of rock in the roof of the tunnel. It crashed down against the door."

"Did it hit you?" Lisa shoved and shoved without shifting the door.

"No. I told you, I'm OK!"

"Lisa, we gotta get him out of there!" Kirstie felt the hairs on her neck prickle as she heard the grunts of the adult bear grow closer. She ran to her friend's side.

"I've shoved all I can. It doesn't work!"

"OK, grab a plank of wood at the bottom edge. It's rotten, see? Try pulling!"

Together, they wrenched at the loose boards. The old wood creaked as it bent, then split with a loud splintering noise. Two long sections of wood came loose in their hands.

"Again!" Lisa gasped. "We take out this whole section and give Stevie room to squeeze through!"

Kirstie nodded. "Before the bears get here!"

"How close are they?"

"Pretty close. If they find Stevie holed up in there, they'll tear the rest of this door right down. He won't stand a chance!"

So they heaved again, forcing the planks out of position until suddenly they split and snapped.

"Now let's see if the gap's big enough!" Kirstie cried, easing her head and shoulders through. The stale air of the tunnel hit her nostrils and almost made her choke. There was pitch darkness, a century of damp and decay. Feeling with her fingertips, she discovered the rockfall that Stevie had told them about, which had piled stones against the shallow entrance.

"Hurry!" It was Lisa's turn to plead from the tangle of brushwood by the entrance.

"Stevie, can you grab my hand?" Kirstie groped in the dark, reaching beyond the pile of rocks. She felt a hand take hold of hers and wrapped her fingers tight around it. Gradually, her eyes were growing used to the dark, and she made out the pale, oval shape of Stevie's face, the white patch of the bandage covering the cut on his forehead.

"Got it!" he whispered.

"OK, now crawl up the heap of rocks... go easy, keep a hold... right!"

He scrambled toward her, stumbling against the fallen rocks, finding footholds, crouching low to avoid the roof, lying flat to wriggle over the top of the pile.

"Keep on coming!" Kirstie showed him there was room to squeeze through. "How are we doing out there?" she called over her shoulder to Lisa.

"Oh, jeez!" The answer came as a terrified sigh.

As Stevie finally scrambled through the tight gap into the daylight and Kirstie turned to see for herself, the bear appeared on the ridge. She was thirty feet from her den, on all fours, hauling herself out of the steep ravine, snapping twigs underfoot as she came.

Kirstie, Stevie, and Lisa cowered by the mine entrance.

The bear saw them: the humans who had invaded her territory. As she drew herself up onto her hind legs, they saw the strong limbs and great, curved claws, the light patch on her chest, the brown, square muzzle.

Then the cubs scrambled onto the ridge behind their mother—a third of her size, more agile, and quicker than the heavy adult. Seeming not to notice the three intruders, they picked at leaves and scraped the ground for tasty roots, tangling themselves in bushes and bumping into tree trunks.

Would the bear attack again? Kirstie crouched and stared at her. Now there was no Johnny or Rocky to rescue them; the horses were twenty paces along the ridge, pulling at their tethers but tied fast. It was up to her. Trembling, hardly able to breathe, she stood up.

The bear watched without reacting.

Kirstie raised both arms wide. She made herself tall, took a step toward the bear along the narrow ridge.

The bear opened her jaws, snapped them shut. Behind her, the cubs played.

Another step, then another. A twig snapped, a bramble caught against her leg...

The bear's small, black eyes blinked. She turned her head toward her cubs.

"Give us five minutes and we're out of here!" Kirstie spoke. What she said wasn't important. It was the sound of her voice that mattered—calm, not threatening. "We'll never get in your way again!"

One of the cubs heard the sound of Kirstie's voice and made a run toward her. The mother stuck out a paw and pushed him back. The cub rolled and scrambled onto his feet.

"Five minutes!" Kirstie repeated. Tall as she could, taking another cautious step, she advanced.

OK! The mother bear made her decision. Swiftly, she rounded up her cubs and herded them off the ridge, down the slope the way they had come. Her huge body crashed through bushes, her feet trampled the undergrowth. The ground shook. She was gone.

10

"No more races!" Lisa begged. "No more fooling around with the Jensens, Stevie, please!"

Kirstie walked behind with Rocky and Johnny, leaving Lisa to sort things out with Stevie Kane. *Give me a nice hot tub!* she said to herself. *Give me a day when nothing goes wrong. And never, ever make me have to face another black bear in the whole of my life!*

"I don't know why I did it in the first place." Stevie hung his head. "It was like Troy said, 'You wanna race?' and I said yes because I couldn't say no, if you see what I mean."

"I know!" Lisa sympathized.

I don't! Kirstie thought, still shaking from the experience. The two horses walked quietly down the hill from Miners' Ridge, saddles creaking, stirrups swaying gently as they plodded for home.

"It wasn't even as if my dad was looking on," Stevie continued. "When he's there, I always have to live up to…"

"…Live up to what you think he wants you to be," Lisa said with a sigh. "Yeah, I know."

"Do you?" He turned to look her in the face.

"Yeah. It's all mixed in with your mom dying, I guess. You want to live up to what your dad wants you to be because it's what you both think your mom would have wanted, too. But I'm not sure that's right. No way would your mom want you to do things you don't want to do, only she's not around to tell you that anymore. Do you see?"

"Yeah…" Stevie said slowly, staring wide-eyed at Lisa.

Amazed by Lisa's long speech, Kirstie tried to puzzle it out. Well, yeah. It all came down to Stevie and his dad not coping…

Lisa's face was covered in blushes, but she was determined to set Stevie straight. "Your mom would

144

want you to do what makes you happy. So what would that be?"

There was a long silence. The leaves of the aspen trees shook, silver and green in the breeze. Overhead, the sky was bright blue.

"Not to be a jockey, for a start." Stevie spoke with a catch in his throat. "I like working with horses back home in Kerry, but I don't want to ride in races and be the winner all the time. It's too much pressure. I'm not good enough."

"So tell your dad," Lisa said. "Tell him you want to ride out on trails, work in the stables, whatever."

They came out of the trees into the valley and the long sweep of green meadow that led to Half Moon Ranch.

"I can't!" The idea made Stevie tense up and shake his head.

"Why not?"

"Because...!"

"Because you'd lose face," Kirstie said quietly.

Lisa and Stevie turned quickly in surprise.

"This is about keeping up an image," she insisted. "It all has to do with your pride."

* * *

"It takes guts to tell the real truth."

This was Lisa's final word on the subject as she, Kirstie, and Stevie approached the ranch.

Paddy Kane came running over the footbridge with Troy and Brad Jensen. The Texan boys took Rodeo Rocky and Johnny Mohawk from Kirstie and led them to the water to drink.

"What happened? Where were you?" Stevie's father took him by the arm. Worry strained his voice, his hand shook as he looked into his son's eyes.

What would it be, Kirstie wondered, *a cover-up or the truth?*

Stevie frowned. Then he tilted his head back with a touch of defiance. "I fell off my horse."

"Rodeo Rocky? The horse threw you?" Paddy Kane fed him the old story line.

"No, I *fell* off!" Stevie insisted. He glanced quickly at Lisa, who stood close by. "I should never have got on him in the first place. I was stupid!"

His father's frown grew deep and puzzled. He noticed Sandy and Matt's car drive through the gate and down the drive. "OK, so we'll forget it this time," he said hastily.

"No, we won't." This was it, Stevie suggested by the tilt of his chin, the determined look in his gray eyes. "I was stupid enough this time to get thrown and get myself attacked by a bear. That meant I got other people involved...put them in danger!"

"OK, OK!" Paddy Kane was all for marching Stevie off to their cabin before Matt and Sandy got out of the car to join them.

"No." Stevie stood his ground. "Lisa and Kirstie rescued me. Without them, I wouldn't be here now!"

Kirstie glanced at Lisa, whose eyes were fixed on Stevie.

"And that's not all!" Stevie saw Sandy and Matt, and his voice grew louder. He didn't care who heard. Let Troy and Brad come close with the horses, let them all hear what he had to say! "The next bit is about my first accident!"

"Later!" Roughly, Paddy Kane pulled him away.

"No, Dad; now. That was my fault, too. I fell, OK? Johnny Mohawk didn't buck me off. There wasn't even a bear to spook him. Nothing. Just me and my bad riding!"

Sandy Scott stopped in her tracks. She hooked

her fingers through the belt loops of her jeans and listened.

"Say that again!" Matt acted like he couldn't believe his ears. "Go ahead, say it!"

"I made Johnny Mohawk go along the track by cutting him with my stick," Stevie told them loud and clear. "No one was looking, so when he still wouldn't go, I kicked him until he did. He lost his footing and started to slide down the hill. I was yelling at him and making things worse. In the end, I lost my balance and fell off. That's it. End of story!"

Yes! Kirstie clenched her fists tight. Johnny Mohawk was innocent. Stevie had admitted it! *Yes, yes!*

Lisa smiled softly at Stevie. Sandy nodded at Matt.

Paddy Kane dropped Stevie's arm and stepped back. Small muscles in his jaw clicked and jumped, his mouth opened but no words came out.

Stevie shook his head as if to say sorry. "And, Dad, I don't want to follow in your footsteps and be a jockey," he whispered so that no one but Lisa, Kirstie, and Paddy Kane could hear him. "There's no way I'd ever be good enough; not if I worked at it for the rest of my life!"

"At a time like that, I guess a man just has to take it," Hadley murmured.

As soon as the wrangler came back from the morning ride, Kirstie had told him word for word what had happened between Paddy and Stevie Kane.

"Paddy said he was sorry!" That was the incredible part: Mr. Kane's face creasing up as if he was in pain after Stevie had said he wasn't good enough, a few seconds of silence, then the words, "Son, I'm sorry!" spilling out of his mouth.

Hadley nodded without stopping work. They were in the corral, checking Johnny Mohawk for cuts and bruises after his latest adventure, before Hadley sent him back to Red Fox Meadow with Kirstie.

"And now there's not gonna be any court case!" Kirstie went on. "No attorneys, no writs to say that the ranch was to blame for Stevie's accident—nothing!"

"Hmm." Hadley lifted Johnny's feet and checked the shoes for sharp stones.

"Mom says it all happened because there was too much pressure. She says the Kanes never meant any harm, not really."

"Hmm."

"She said we just had to wait until they came to their senses."

"That Troy kid, and his big brother, did they say *they* were sorry?" Hadley asked. He slipped a head collar onto Johnny and handed the lead rope over to Kirstie.

"No way!" she laughed. "They're eating lunch right now, planning another race with Charlie!"

"What did Charlie say?"

"He said, 'Why not practice some tricks for Saturday's rodeo instead?'" Kirstie had caught this before she came across to the corral. The Saturday event was the way they always rounded off a week's activities on the ranch. "He promised to teach them some new ones. But not on Johnny Mohawk and Rodeo Rocky. He told them the horses needed to rest."

"Good for Charlie," Hadley grunted. "So you're OK?"

Kirstie's eyebrows shot up; Hadley never asked

you if you were OK because he always supposed you were. "I'm fine."

"And Lisa; she's OK?"

Kirstie grinned. "She's great!" Kirstie still couldn't get over the way her friend had handled Stevie.

Hadley nodded and tipped back his hat. "So take the horse to the meadow."

"C'mon, Johnny!" Kirstie said, leading the horse out into the yard with the sun beating down and across the bridge onto the soft green turf.

Linda and Carole Holgate sat on the riverbank in shorts and bare feet, waving at Kirstie and Johnny as they went by. Ahead, leaning on the fence by Red Fox Meadow, Lisa and Stevie stood deep in conversation.

"Hey, Lisa!" she called.

"Hey, Kirstie!"

Stevie ran to open the gate.

"Thanks, Stevie." She smiled and nodded. Their eyes made warm contact. Everything had worked out fine.

She was through the gate and Johnny was already thinking of all the grass and clover he would eat. His head was up, his neck making that amazing arc. He was tossing his black mane, high-stepping into the meadow, impatient for Kirstie to take off the collar.

For a few seconds, she held on to the rope. After all, she'd almost lost him.

Until Stevie told the truth.

Not that Kirstie had ever doubted Johnny Mohawk. She let him go now with a swift movement to unbuckle the head collar. He ducked his beautiful head and slipped away, gathered speed, and galloped like a dream.

ABOUT THE AUTHOR

Born and brought up in Harrogate, Yorkshire, Jenny Oldfield went on to study English at Birmingham University, where she did research on the Brontë novels and on children's literature. She then worked as a teacher before deciding to concentrate on writing. She writes novels for both children and adults and, when she can escape from her desk, likes to spend time outdoors. She loves the countryside and enjoys walking, gardening, playing tennis, riding, and traveling with her two daughters, Kate and Eve.